Dedicated to my mother, father and brother. And to my whole extended family, the best people I know.

CHAPTER 1

This isn't the first time I have chased her. The last time was through the forest. Before that, across a bay. I swam. She had a boat. Now she glides across the extraterrestrial terrain, her yellow jumpsuit clear as the sun against the darkness of space.

When she jumps over the last crater, she disappears. This plateau, pockmarked and uneven, has to end somewhere. I walk through the crater, slowly reaching the edge. I gaze below. A full drop, hundreds of feet to the ground.

"Down here, dummy." I look for where the voice comes from but can't see anything.

"Where are you?" I say. Thirty feet below me, a red towel flies out of the serrated side of the plateau. Her hand waves from an unseen alcove in the steppe. I notice a ladder carved down the rock wall, sections ground down conveniently to provide each step.

"Don't be a baby, you strong man, you. Drop after the last step and don't look back," she teases. I take the risk and begin to lower myself down the side of the rock wall. Reaching the bottom of the ladder, I play along, release my hands, and drop on the last step.

She catches my feet and pulls me into the chamber. It is roomier than I expected. But she doesn't give me the chance to inspect the quarters. She draws me to her body and examines my face, her hand tracing my nose and cheeks.

"They were rough with you. They are rough sometimes." She kisses my right cheek and turns me around to face the ledge. She steps in front of me. Both my arms rest around her shoulders.

We stare at the blue-and-green sphere. The rotation of the earth occurs before our eyes. From this point it looks like it will never end. On the planet I can never feel the endless pull east. Yet from this location, 1,070 miles per hour looks oddly fast. I stare at her face, the narrow chin twitching nervously.

"I love our games, Adri. But I don't like the game." My hand runs across her jaw line.

"Do you know where we will be in a few years?" she asks.

"No," I say. The western hemisphere sits in plain view. I extend my left arm and point my hand towards the Pacific, the edge of California. I give her a questioning look.

"Wrong," she says flatly.

I point towards the eastern coastline, the Gulf of Mexico.

"How could you?" she admonishes. She raises her hand to control my arm. I keep my finger pointing outwards. She avoids

North America entirely, and South America. My hand extends outwards from the globe to an empty patch of space near the moon.

"There?"

Nodding her head in confirmation, she squeezes my hand. I feel a shaking in my body and my hand twitches, my neck spasms, and I feel convulsions in my back muscles. My vision begins to obscure. Everything flashes blue.

CHAPTER 2

SEVERAL WEEKS EARLIER...

Last night was so different. A normal night filled with paperwork and millions of unanswered requests. My work has streamlined a lot in the past ten years. When I went to law school I spent a cool grand on books every semester. I still have the books but they're for show and show only. Now I can cross-reference thousands of cases by simply shouting random topics to my automated law clerk/secretary, Dorothy. I don't type e-mails anymore. I just see the work each day. So instead of playing tag with another attorney in snail mail and e-mail, this synthetic personality cuts through the cheese for me AND answers the phones. Way better than the $15-an-hour kids I used to hire. But since I can work faster I take more work and the load is a bit much. I'm three weeks behind on work that will take three months, or if you want, too fucking reckless with my web-advertising money.

I sleep four to five hours a night now. But it's OK. I stopped losing my hair about four years ago, so really, it's OK. I remember in 2012 when the England striker celebrated a goal by pretending to hairspray his recent ass-to-face hair transplant, all smooth and seductive as a bulldog in full gallop. It was like spiking a flat top, a part lacking a part line. Atrocious, laughable worldwide. But I felt for the guy. I'm deathly afraid of losing my hair. I have some white hairs but I have the same parted waviness I did when I was younger. Even with my ex's repeated attempts to remind me I will never be who I was when I was twenty-three. No shit, babe. I don't want to be.

Simplicity leads to happiness. But happiness is an art. I learned that when I was eighteen. I wasn't very smart back then because I thought that the most complex situations could be worked out. I thought, and still think, anything can be forgiven. It was a shield I wore, a guard for my psyche. The wife broke down the guard for years until she decided that our life was not enough. Julia left the mortgage and took the dog, moving less for work and more for inheritance. Chasing destiny is one thing, chasing dollars for sense is another. Since then my sword is in the sheath, meeting a new partner a mere afterthought, and each week oscillates between alcoholism and teetotaling.

I digress. Let's go back to yesterday. Another great day in the life. I'd already ordered in and the salad place downstairs is relatively fast. I had three clients in the evening but I had to do some real work before then. She teleconferenced me unannounced. Urgent.

"Roger, I know you don't want to talk to me, but I want you to get rid of the gun."

"Why?" I asked, picking at my Chinese chicken salad. She looked at me like I was too unhinged to understand. "You know I never fire it, Julia."

"Still, you have it and I would feel better if it was somewhere else." She looked bored by the whole thing. Chewing gum and twiddling with her hair, like she was being watched.

"OK. I'll sell it back to the store." A princess gets what she wants. The pauper fights for what he needs. I bent over and lit up off camera, then returned, the cigarette comfortably off the screen.

"When did you start smoking again, Roger?"

"How did you know, Jules?"

"I've heard you light a cigarette about a thousand times."

"Oh." I hung up, swiped over to my doc processor, and worked as fast as I could. The client meetings were painful and I couldn't turn off my thoughts. We haven't spoken in two months and she calls me to say this? Terrible. So I woke up this morning with a bottle of Beam in my bed and the neighbor's cat trapped in the condo, murdering the *Carmina Burana* for a good two hours. I didn't mind.

I always look forward to sleep on Fridays but this one is extra-special. It's a guaranteed eight hours. After all, I paid for it. Drug and alcohol free for one night. When I approach the bed tonight, strip down to my skivvies, and push the button that tucks me in, I'm already satisfied. They push my hands as deep as possible into the blanket each time. The toxic heat of the blanket feels absolutely fantastic. It's just pleasant.

CHAPTER

But then I wake up. My senses are acute, on fire, stimulated to an almost wild enjoyment. My nose picks up familiarity, sensual notes. Cardamom and bergamot filter into my body, my olfactory system alight. The bed is covered in a web of white knitted cotton and thick linens. Like they were made in some loom, stitched out of necessity. Almost an envelope for my body. The breeze is hot when I lift my hand in the air and see the sunlight pour onto my arms, hairs singed to attention. It's fucking bright here. I lower my hand and feel the bed, cold as if a butler hung the sheets outside a mountain cabin. I push the heavy wooden window closed. The effect seals the room and ends my blindness.

Nothing here is mine. I can't find my credit stick, identifier, or glasses. But my vision is fine so I guess I'm wearing my contacts. I see the Virgin of Guadalupe on the other side of the room; her merciful gaze projects itself above me. The ceiling and walls are adobe with the wooden frame exposed, held together by crude yet effective architecture. Like one of the many missions put together over three hundred years ago. Sage burns in the corner. Books line the wall opposite me and paintings of religious icons and scenes are everywhere. I stare at the ceiling and see a watercolor rendition of the sky. The colors blend together, a jubilant accompaniment of cherubs and heavens. The fiery heat, sweltering from outside, has dissipated into a cool dryness. I feel at home.

I hear water in my periphery, somewhere to the far left of my head and reverberating off the wood and tile floors. Something moves to the left of me but my eyes only see one thing. An abused paperback of *Infantry Attacks* breathes into the air. Pages contract and heave from the sudden pressure fluctuation and conveniently fall. To a damn good page. One of my favorites. *The battle raged in undiminished fury and almost without interruption into the late afternoon. For the third time I ordered ammunition and hand grenades replenished in the front line. Through the smoke clouds of our heavy shells....*

That's getting really good so I have to put it down. His writing is hypnotic, persuasive. I mean, you're reading a man who has to make snap decisions for thousands of lives. The tides of war turn with each word. And against that persistent flux of the water... just magic. The water calms and transforms the prose, an added eccentricity. But someone is playing with it. Erratic and impulsive, like putting your thumb in the hose or a toe in the bathtub, enjoying the flow of water under mechanical control.

And it's her again, lightly humming in the tub. I've known her for months... it must be months at this rate. And even as I've gotten older I have the juvenile, young man reaction. It's too damn predictable nowadays. It must be the cadence of her voice. The arm outstretched in the air, content to float in the air. And the song... it's a piano version and I recognize the melody but not the words just yet. I know they will come to me. For whatever reason I cannot recognize the song at all. It's as unrecognizable as a black star collapsing in my mind. Let's just blame it on the satellites instead.

I can breathe easy now and time starts to fly. The music, the hand gliding through the air, the crescendo of her voice against the unforgettable melody. Off a wooden side-stand she grabs a book and flips through it, humming away. This pleasure is reckless. For whatever reason, I just figured out I could actually leave the goddamn bed. I don't really want to. I guess this situation could end even better.

So I will lay in this bed and let her read so we can enjoy this moment.

For a while.

How can you not let time pass when movement could only impede the flow?

Anyways, it's better when she asks for me.

"Rooggggggyyyyyyeerrrrrrrrrrrrrr"

"Yes?"

"You know, I cannot seduce you more." She gives me the finger. I laugh, hyperventilating at the end.

"I know. I love it."

"I must agree. I love it too." She flexes her hand in the doorway, her knuckles folding into her skin as she stretches. "Do you really want me to do more to make you come here?" she asks.

"Not really," I reply.

"Yes you do."

"No. I mean what more could I want?" And when I say that her hand disappears for a few seconds. No hand returns. A red towel flies out of the bathroom to fall halfway on the bed. "OK. OK." A tease.

"That was your towel, you know. Mine is blue."

"Really?" And a blue towel follows the flight pattern of the red one. A kamikaze chasing after an unfinished job. I cannot stop laughing.

"Alright, alright. You win." And I get out of the bed for the last time. I grab both of the towels and throw them over my shoulder and walk into the bathroom. The water rests comfortably over her breasts and she stares at me – she's been staring ever since I set foot in the damn room. I meet her eyes as fast as I can and give her the same treatment as I walk on each and every tile until I find a nice spot to sit. As far away from her as possible.

"Well," she mutters.

"Well... this sure is beautiful isn't it." It couldn't get better.

"It couldn't get better, Roger." Except for her dissatisfaction, which right now is a huge point of my pleasure. If she's a tease, then I'm the jester.

"Do you want to try it?"

"Yes."

"OK."

She steps out of the water and pretends to grab the towel while she shuffles in front of the mirror. Her weight shifts to her left leg as she shoves the door closed. She stands for about two or three minutes. Steam emanates off her whole body, magnified into water droplets by the cold dampness of the room, raining on the mirror. At this point there is no reflection.

I drop the towels and go to stand directly behind her. I take her hand and move it right over her reflection. In this sweltering heat, the fog covering the mirror seems to turn a rosy pink.

My hand guides her hand to the mirror and I start tracing her index finger through the steam.

W H E R E R U

And she pushes me with her butt and turns around with a coy smile. She makes a victory symbol with two fingers. Then throws down an E. And then curls her hand, creating an N or an R, I can't really tell. Apparently this is just another thing I can't control on this planet.

W H A T I S U R N A

I laugh and nod with a deliberate recklessness to key her in, trying to seem as normal as possible.

This isn't a normal Friday night. But it's supposed to be.

The mirror flashes blue. Everything just flashed blue. The lights go off entirely. The darkness petrifies and I have lost control of my muscles.

FOREIGN WATERS

Thankfully, I wake up. The bed is still cool, almost as if I haven't slept in it. I feel great, relaxed, refreshed, brimming with energy. Almost too much energy. I am so used to exhaustion that, well, eight more hours makes a big difference.

***

"Good morning, sir," he says. He takes my hand and holds it as I move slowly out of the pod. I can't feel his hands. Or the temperature in the room. It feels like half my body is still asleep, each touch fuzzy and indefinite. He hands me a glass of green juice from my food tray. The cup of Earl Grey looks ready, the egg-white omelette has the right amount of grease. I chug the juice, a refinement of poly-proteins and amino acids with a lovely orange flavor.

"Good morning, Jim. How is the weather outside?"

"It's tipping 131 but there is a cool breeze from the ocean. No fog this morning. In the shade it's about 112. Your car, of course, has been kept in the garage at a cool 77 degrees."

"Thanks, Jim. I love hearing that."

"Of course, Mr. Escobar. We aim to please. But I have to inform you that you committed more than one violation during the session."

"What do you mean?"

"Customers are not allowed to communicate with other customers about their lives outside of the evening, sir. Attempting to do so also augments the program in ways outside of the terms of service. That was your first violation – the attempt at communication. Your other infractions stem from the aforementioned term-of-service violations." Service Attendant Jim smiles. Of course. The terms of service. How could I ever forget those 150 pages of my life ripped away from me. Intricate traps to absolve the company from liability. Muddy logic in five different languages. Rules and stuff. I could die. Blah blah blah.

"I don't understand. Honestly."

"Sir, we have had this conversation before." The attendant snickers. "Our company is designed to optimize your experience at all moments, at all times, provided you work within the parameters of the program. The coding language allows you to exhibit free will as long as it is, umm, within the script. Your infractions are not more clever than our code."

"I left the script?"

"It doesn't matter if you left the script or she left the script. Simply leaving the script stretches the code and, if I may, cheapens the product. Look. You're mixing Sprite into your Champagne. Let the program work for you and it will only get better, I promise." He taps his tablet and stares at the number of infractions I have. "Sir, you have one official warning left, unless you want to save it. Your current penalty is two weeks."

"I'll take the warning." This is the nineteenth time Jim and I have done this ritual but the first time I've been warned about a penalty. Whatever. I grin and walk to the restroom. The shower here is better than the one in the apartment. I turn it on and the water scalds my face. I lower it slowly to cool my skin to retain feeling. I really can't afford to lose this place to such a petty desire. I need next week.

So I have to show I'm content or else this is over. To tell you the truth, it's easy to be content here. My shoes and suit wait for me this bright Saturday morning, polished and dry-cleaned to perfection. The product here has always been great, a point of obsession for me. I have to be honest. Not only does your suit get pressed but their tailor does some wonders on the loose ends you didn't know you had. They'll even touch up your glasses, visors, and linens for free. Membership was expensive, but that! That is a good deal.

The dead heat of summer rolled into the valley three days ago. This shamelessly coincided with the nucloud's orbit, plunging the city into a fiery inferno. Ultimately no one can go outside for more than ten, fifteen minutes without visors and a full set of linens. The city felt particularly unlucky. When the Lakers got swept by the Suns it was poetic justice that no fan could really bear. So most of my friends are content to watch movies and miniseries for the next three weeks. Misery loves company. And couches.

But Jane and Murph said they wanted to take the boat out and fish for a few hours and that sounds like a great idea. The fish are ready to jump. I'll be ready.

CHAPTER

IV

When I wake up in the hospital this morning I am confused. I remember the car arriving last night and the guy from the dealership handing me the keys. My intention was to rest before work, sleep, and watch reruns of old television shows that reminded me of college. I should have dozed off in a haze. Yet here I am, in the hospital, watching a few med students delicately remove shards of fiberglass and Teflon from my left side and leg.

But too much sleep means too much to think about. My mind took advantage of this time alone to come up with new ways to curse me. The torment of the past few hours was through repressed memories. Maybe the painkillers created visions from my subconscious. Jules stares me down, her hips saddling my body, her arm extending to pull back her hair and tossing it into a ponytail with a sinister, seductive smile. Her fingers rattle on the cell phone while I cook, a disinterested beauty sitting on the couch. The then-limited affection drips away like fat from the chops. These scenes persisted for most of my sleep. Fifteen hours wasted, woken by anger. I can't get paid for them, I can't write it off. I'm stuck.

"You don't look so great, buddy." My eyes are hazy and reckless. I can't tell a tit from a scalpel. The voice rouses me out of the mental affliction, an effort to raise me from my sleep. They must have added a stimulant to the drip feed to bring me back. A glance around reveals that I've been in the ER for more than a few hours. Bloody gloves sit in the sink. The clock says it's about 3 p.m. Three med students crowd around my lower abdomen, my thighs exposed. Some shards had punctured my quadricep through and through. It seems like a delicate procedure. A glasses-encumbered nerd lifts my skin apart, hoisting the long shard of fiberglass in my leg to the air. My muscles involuntary twitch. My bone itself is exposed as they elevate the muscle into an easier work space. A hot assistant sprays my leg with some fluid, maybe a pain suppressant or cell disperser, and the third, an oafish man child, handles the tweezers to gently remove each needle-wide sliver out and dump it into a box. A box filling with blood.

"Yeah, this is a good day for me. How long have you guys been at this?"

"Six hours. You've been out for fifteen. Apparently you fell asleep behind the wheel." The girl says. They show me an accident report. My sleepy head guided the steering wheel and myself and that brand new Caddy into the center divider. Nobody else was injured. Somehow toxicology found little alcohol in my system. The report says I lost consciousness at impact but I think I lost consciousness long before then. Whole sequences of events exist outside of my ability to remember. The med students giggle as they watch me flip through the whole thing, like a secret conversation. "So... do you go out much?" the hot one says. She smiles, her cheeks barely hidden by her mask.

"That's enough now, guys. Just stay focused." From the voice from behind me. My senses are still numb and I cannot pick apart if it's a man or a woman. But when the hand rests on my shoulder it could be only one person. John Murphy, Murph's dad. I must be at the county hospital. His volunteer time. Great. He sits at the side of my bed and stares into my eyes, his retinas obfuscated by the deep concave curve in his glasses. "It's nice to see you, Roger."

"Great to see you too, John, like always. Sad it has to be..." and I point at the three dimwits attending to my leg, "like this."

"Hey, bad things happen to good people. Just be glad you're alive, and well, so is everyone else." He smiles.

"Yeah. How did I look when I got in?"

"I was here when you got in. You looked like shit. This is actually pretty good improvement over the past...." He looks at his watch. "Fifteen hours."

"Glad to hear I'm doing good, Doctor John." He smiles when I say that. His eyes turn soft.

"Maybe it's a good thing she isn't in your life anymore, Roger."

"Who?"

"You know who. You can't shut up about her."

"Hey, Doc, I haven't mentioned her once." The med students laugh.

"Yeah, since you've been awake." He furrows his brow. "This isn't healthy for you. You've never really been a drinker, a doper, or even a retail-therapy type of guy. But it's been three years, Roger. That's more than a thousand days."

"I've moved on. I'm seeing someone else."

"That's bullshit. She moved on. And you can't shut up about her while you're asleep. Who are you kidding."

He can't be telling me this because he wants to, that much is for sure. John is a surgeon. A clinician. His people skills have never been the best. Even when he shared a beer with me at graduation, a simple clap on the shoulder and a speech about duty was all I got. At my wedding he mostly beamed and took photos for his wife. There's a reason he worked with doped-up, unconscious people. Nobody can talk back. He likes his own conversation.

I shift my other leg and lightly smack the oaf with my feet.

"The less you move the better. I worked on this for five hours last night and, while I gave it my best and these kids are doing a great job, you're going to need at least a week of recovery. If you can work from home, great, just don't see clients. But you'll be on several analgesics and have to apply that healing spray that Judy keeps using to make sure you don't get scar tissue. Even a little scar accumulation, in that muscle, could cripple you. By the way, you won't be walking till Friday."

"So I have to shit in a pan and sleep in a chair?" I ask.

"Just what the doctor ordered." He grins as the serious look leaves his face. He places his hand on my shoulder, squeezes it, and walks out of the room. I ask the students to dope me out for at least a little bit and they comply.

Strangely, the sleep is fine. I wake up at home, my nostrils filled by the scents of coffee and bacon fat. I forgot the great thing about universal health care – my own attendant. Better than Jim at T.D.S. or the one at work. I hope she's hot, and if not, it's OK. Eggs, bacon, and coffee.

This is going to be a great week.

CHAPTER

Not surprisingly, the lost Monday and now Tuesday has put me hopelessly behind. I had Heather, my government-mandated attendant and nurse, go to the office to switch my digital assistant to a new setting that I hadn't used before. It's not vacation mode, in case you were wondering. Instead of rejecting all new clients, I enabled Dorothy's auto-referral script into live mode. Now clients got sent to my former coworkers/friendly attorneys via a cheery message from this digital avatar, who proclaimed: Mr. Escobar will work for you, even if he cannot be present here today. Please, let me make this introduction. I wish I was that cordial. I get 25 percent of each case they take. This, of course, is a win/win. My father always said that the best job is one where you make money while you are asleep. In my case, on painkillers.

Heather is so funny around the condo. Well, maybe not funny. Maybe I'm just not used to the presence of a woman so willing to organize and clean up a mess that I find acceptable. I set her up in our guest room, which, for whatever reason, has not been used for several years. The once immaculate space morphed from a family condo to a workplace in the past few years. I hadn't put a flower in a vase for years. The champagne flutes and fancy plates haven't been used since

Jules left. Heather took one look at the dust, furrowed her brow, and got to work. Even though it cracked 115 degrees today she opened the windows. I put the central air on full blast.

"If I'm gonna make you healthy, well, we're gonna at least make it smell decent in here." She was from the South. Her accent gave it away. From Kentucky, if I had to wager. The hand gestures, the sly curl of lip upon each slurred word. She gave a smile of one who enjoys the process of taking care of an object, person, or place. It was less about control and more about preserving the peace. Her peace. The job of public servants, well, THESE public servants, was not only to keep the patient but themselves healthy. Government workers of this type were given the liberty to make wholesale changes to their living environments for the duration of their stay. It was a tough job, one of the toughest, but the pay was good. Plus four months of vacation... how can you beat that?

"So are we burning candles now?"

"Candles? Come on now. You look so down and out we should probably burn sage and call a medicine man." She laughed. I had to smile.

"No seriously. I don't want any of that peach mango sherbert stuff they sell at Target. Or anything named 'vanilla.' Something alive is better."

"Flowers?"

"Sure. And cook whatever you think is good. I trust you."

"Well you have to trust me, I'm changing your diapers."

"I will." We had made peace. The condo won't look the same in a few days, I know it. I'm not a crude man but I know this place has been a cave for months. I had saved newspapers from the last Lakers championship, the World Cup, and the election. Bankers boxes filled with unorganized depositions, medicals, and needless notes. People like her don't let rot and decay fester, especially when they are paid to clean it up.

Still there were huge drawbacks from the accident. Not just the caseload buildup, that was to be expected. Missed appointments evolved into big mistakes, and big mistakes mean emergency provisions will be taken. I don't like to talk too much about my work or let anyone else know much more beyond the names. But I guess Heather will have to know. Thank goodness that most of the information is now publicly available so as to avoid confidentiality issues. I sat her down to give her an introduction to my client and largest headache, Cruz Romero.

He became a client when my friend Arthur introduced me to him years ago. I was a younger man then and, when Arthur and I took a business trip to Mexico City, Romero made a point to show us a devilishly good time. The marbles I lost on that trip are still lost, probably in some seedy alley I have long chosen to forget.

FOREIGN WATERS

Born in Sinaloa, Mexico, Romero moved to the states about a decade ago. He came from money. This was when the border finally broke. Illegal immigration was at an all-time low, and the United States was practically begging people to bring money into the country. So Romero dropped half a million into the farmland around Peoria, Illinois. He started an agricultural development company to provide cheaper greenhouse materials for lower-income farmers. It was a clean deal. Peoria was badly hit by the second depression and he managed to create four hundred jobs in under a year and a half, at least fifty of them above the poverty line. He got an EB-5 visa in the process. Thirty years ago it would have taken him twenty years to become a citizen. It took Romero ten days.

Yet nothing is as it seems. Remember when the the federal government of Mexico buckled under the weight of the cartels? Each of the Mexican states were fine but corruption had reached the top, resulting in murders near the apex of the Mexican federal government. The U.N. intervened to dismantle the system and placed Mexico City under multinational rule.

To end violence, the U.N. granted an absurd resolution. Coming clean as to their associates, the associated cartels could gain legitimate business status in Mexico as pharmaceutical companies and deal in a legal drug trade. Of course, the violence had to stop, the bribery had to stop, and the government had to be restored.

In exchange for allowing the cartels to gain corporate status (and engage in international trade), the United States needed to get something in return. After all, this meant billions of dollars could now legitimately leave our deficit-ridden country. As part of the compromise, much of the jungles in southern Mexico were purchased by Uncle Sam and sold to the major agricultural conglomerates. High temperatures had ravaged the American Midwest. Crop production was down and famine was near. But the jungles, some of the few places left that didn't need a greenhouse to grow crops, evolved into the new farmland. The new fifty-second state was comprised of Veracruz, Campeche, and Merida, all lands that used to be run by the cartels. They were still there, secretly, engaged in business. But for all practical purposes the land was American, as were the soybeans, corn, and rice produced alongside each crop of narcotics.

In disclosing this information and losing their land power, many of the cartels created holding companies to protect their illegal brands. Mostly in the form of pharmaceutical or agricultural entities on both sides of the border, they dubbed some lower-ranked employees their "shareholders" to preserve the anonymity of their "investors." But to breed fear, the companies were named after dead leaders, much like how a president will get state parks or libraries. It was narco-capitalism at its finest. The drugs began to flow freely, taxable and all, over the border, a pestilence upon the lower class. It was like the end of Prohibition. While cocaine, heroin, and meth were still popular, a synthesized, highly addictive version of ayahuasca mixed with a variety of designer drugs gained street cred. I'd see it down on Skid Row almost daily. The loony bin was let out, everyone was a preacher.

That's where the public information had to stop. You didn't need a military clearance or sign some nondisclosure forms to find out this information, even when the papers stopped reporting on the "little" developments. Like how the owners and shareholders of these corporations were executed left and right. This is where meeting people like Romero revealed the truth.

"Ohhhhhhhhhhh," she said, with feigned excitement. I put a finger to her lip and continued.

Then came Operation "Mas Que Nada." A play on words and ideas, really, and only hinted at by the news conglomerates. By acquiring the identity of 90 percent of the cartels' families, the CIA and the FBI brought the blood war right at them. It wasn't so much an assassination campaign, but more a mass execution. The news called it vigilante activity, the blame pushed upon the American "Don't Tread On Me" attitude. In under a month, the three major cartels lost 85 percent of their workforce due to casualties. Ten percent simply vanished, probably to Gitmo. Five months later the U.N. resolution was abolished, the Mexican government was reestablished, and drug rehab clinics across the United States were packed with junkies without a fix.

How does all this have to do with Romero? He was a mechanical engineer in Mexico. Most of his money looked clean from his years of work with Monsanto. Yet several months ago he received a call from Banco Popular in Mexico, which asked what to do with the excess interest in one of his accounts. It seems that he had reached a depositing cap at the bank and the funds needed to be moved out of it. He had no idea where this money came from. So he went to Guadalajara to visit the branch that had received all of it. They informed him that an account had been set up in his name that received deposits from Callatero LLC. The owner of Callatero was an uncle of his who had "passed away" thirteen years ago in Sinaloa. In the same month of the CIA activity. Money trickled in, the fifth of every month. The interest had overflowed the $750,000 limit in ten years. That money needed to go somewhere else.

I warned him to not touch the account. Using some quick math, the interest spillover must have come from a trust of more than four million U.S. dollars. We created a charity for the spillover money, spaying and neutering dogs and cats across Mexico. Romero was a real dog anyways, so the joke was on everybody. The less he touched it, the better it looked. We would fully cooperate with the feds in order to save his visa and, in turn, his citizenship. Possibly his life as well.

He didn't listen. He took a chunk of cash and flew to the Canary Islands. He must have deposited some, gambled some, and spent the rest on hookers and drugs. The man can party. No doubt about that.

And thus, during my fantastic recovery in which Heather, the best nurse ever, fed me real pig bacon, farm-fresh organic eggs, and free-trade coffee, Romero had returned to the States late Sunday night. To L.A., for whatever reason. Tanned, bloated, hung over, probably unable to look out of his sunglasses. His accent never helped him with locals even though most of them have accents as well. I have no doubts as to his intoxication as he couldn't give the Customs and Border Protection agents a reason for his trip to the Canary Islands. By this time the feds had been alerted to his status. Locking him up was an easy call. He spent two days in jail before Arthur called me. I had to make an appearance to get him out, post the bail money, all that good stuff. Somehow I had to get to San Diego, to the CCA Detention Center, and get Romero out before Friday evening. Or he's out of the country.

CHAPTER

VI

I saw an improvement in my leg almost overnight. The cell disassociator did a great job to prevent scar tissue. I normally never miss appointments. Or forget about them. But Romero's was on Tuesday, the day I never left my apartment.

Or really did anything that important. I didn't even check my schedule. Instead, I wake up to the best breakfast in years. We open the bandages. Play with the pieces of skin that had not fully attached yet. Picked away chunks of foam between my leg hairs. Filled a bathtub with tea tree oil. I take a nice long bath, the water slowly remove all the gunk and healing salves. For a bunch of knucklehead med students they were no slouches. The leg looked better. It didn't feel better – what I could feel of it, at least. But the skin looked and felt real, not a graft sewn on for vanity and comfort. I stuck my little finger into the fresh skin tissue, pink and taunt as if it had been grown out of a lab. It looked good.

Thus, this Wednesday morning I awoke to vast conflicts. My regime was simple: no extraneous movement, a good diet, some physical therapy on Thursday and Friday, and by Saturday I should be able to walk. Maybe with a cane. And by Monday I would be able to conduct work normally. When I was unconscious, Doc checked my blood pressure and what Heather called my "stress signs." Aside from the bags under my eyes, the stress had physically degraded my body to a point where the accident appeared inevitable. Overworked, underslept, underfed, and still dealing with a ghost of a woman in my life. It made too much sense to just call it a week.

But I can't let down Arthur. Hell, I can't let down myself. I can't shirk responsibility. It's not talent that got me where I am today. It was hard work, dedication, and a willingness to be focused on the details no one else looked at. Romero is that detail, the corner in my painting of work. Without it the whole balancing act will crumble, slowly, and I suddenly won't care about anything. Jules told me that my biggest problem was that I was too hard on myself, even in those years where laziness became a bigger agenda than passion. Idleness, then, was an art form. This isn't me being too hard on myself, though. This is something she would never do – compromise herself for someone else.

So we'll make it to San Diego today, regardless. I won't be able to sit still here anyways. I want to make a promise to Heather. I stare at her, from the toes up. She's fit for the job.

"If you wanted to check me out, Roger…" She puckers up her lips and pushes her blonde hair back behind her head into a ponytail. She isn't drop-dead gorgeous, a classic American. But just gorgeous enough for a few seconds to consider her for a different job.

"No, I'm not. Just seeing if you can drive."

"Of course I can drive."

"But I drive an old car."

"What's the car?"

"An R8. I'll show you how to drive it."

"How old? I've never heard of it."

"It's an Audi. They aren't in the States anymore, and I guess I got it fifteen years ago. It still runs on gas, but it's the only car I have right now. You'll have to use a steering wheel that really works and wheels not locked into the grid. It's not an easy thing to drive if you've never driven it before, but it's fast."

"I'm not supposed to let you leave."

"You're also supposed to fluff my pillow more, but I'm letting it slide."

"So nice, Roger."

"I'm kidding. But seriously. I need you to drive this car for me. I have…. I mean, I must get down to San Diego. It's work related. I know it's against the rules, but if I don't do this…"

"Someone will go to jail?"

"Well, try lose his citizenship and maybe his life."

"What do you do again?"

"I'm a lawyer."

"People die in jail?"

"Alllll the time, sweetheart. All the time."

We dawdle around for a few minutes, make smaller chit chat and joke about ways you can die in jail. When she realized what was at stake she began to get the leg ready for movement again. This meant a fresh cast, sealed to balance the plethora of delicate variables to properly heal a muscle. It would have to last five to six hours and make me not look like a hack immigration attorney. Crippled, yes. But not another ambulance-chasing vulture. Anything to let me swing a little bit of weight around the place.

Heather places a clear thin sheet, like a piece of clingy aluminum foil, around that part of the leg. Once satisfied, she procured from her bag of tricks a gauze marked "BODY STEEL – 700 UTS." Several wraps around my leg later, she applies a red solution and then blow-dries it. It quickly hardens, a forced relaxation into immobility. Ten minutes later she knocks it with her fist.

"Feels good?"

"I don't feel anything."

She grinned at me and grabbed a frying pan. "You sure?"

"Yup." She brought down the pan on my leg with a force and intensity I have only seen in late-night infomercials. The pan struck the cast and clattered out of her hands, a skipping stone across the floor. The echo reverberated throughout the apartment as our eyes followed the pan to its final rest under the coffee table on the far side of the room.

"When do you want to leave?" she asked.

"Let me call Murph. He has an A-pass."

"You know people with A-passes?"

"Not willingly."

"I'm willing to meet those people, you know."

"Well this was just by circumstance. When your best friend's dad is the king of surgery in the county, these things come our way. Plus if we didn't have the A-pass, would you really want to drive me all the way down to San Diego?"

"Yeah, gimps aren't scary. Sorry, bub."

"Exactly." I dial up Murph. He has no problem with it. His dad had told him all about the accident, even the gory details he neglected to tell me. How when the highway patrol found my car tattered up northbound on the 110, a clear foam coated my mouth. How my lower neck, around my collarbone, looked more like an artist's palate than healthy skin. How they had to give me three bags of insulin to get my hydration levels back up. Still nobody knows why I was in the car in the first place or what caused the accident. The car sensors revealed nothing out of the ordinary except a slow rotation of the wheels towards the center divider, the front piece of the car shredding like fiberglass cheese into a concrete grater. Regardless, Murph wouldn't travel much this week so I could take the pass for a few days.

"Why take the R8, man?" he asks, confused.

"It's the only car I really have. It'll be uncomfortable but that Caddy is toast and the Jetta needs work done. That shitty transmission doesn't exactly speed up the trip, ya know?"

"Yeah, I feel you. If you had to just take the 5 down there you'd be picked off before you even reached Capistrano."

"Yeah, man. I can see the headlines already: 'Beautiful nurse savagely beaten in Newport, lawyer innocently looks on.'" I hide under my blanket a little bit when I said that with hopes that she didn't think I couldn't help her. But I wouldn't help her – I would be stuck in the passenger's seat, a band of savages at arm's reach of the car as we sped through the old suburban jungles of Orange County. We would be sitting ducks in the inevitable "rush hour" traffic of the California highway system. This was commonplace. No one would write about us. Just mere statistics in a grand scheme.

"Don't worry, I'll scrape you up off the concrete," Murph offers.

"Thanks, man. When can you drop off the pass?"

"Whenever you want, hombre."

"Soon?"

"How about now instead?" The phone clicks. I peek over the covers to receive a stern yet playful glare.

"He'll be here soon?" asks Heather.

"Sure. Well, however long it takes in traffic from the beach. That man is as automated as a Rolex." We decide to plan out the next few hours of our life as Murph drove up the freeway into downtown. Traffic would be murderous on a Wednesday – when isn't it murderous, really – but you gotta do what you gotta do. Meanwhile I made Heather make the wheelchair situation look good. It would take a degree of skill to lodge my body into a small sports car such as the R8.

We spend the idle time trying to be less idle. I call the men downstairs to put my car in the handicapped loading spot. I have to acceptable, though. It takes close to forty-five minutes to put on a suit (or at least two pieces of my three-piece suit) over my relatively immobile body. I have to accept that I won't be able to relieve myself for at least four or five hours. So less water and more dopey drugs to keep me catatonic. I start my prep work as we get ready. A friend had transferred to me a guide to negotiations with the Customs and Border Protection Agency, especially at this location. It doesn't seem like it has to be an intimidation job or a "play by the rules you set" sort of confrontation. It is far simpler, more economical. Like the bureaucracy has sorted itself out to be more efficient. Present proper identification documents, retina scans, and what have you. With any luck Romero will be walking free by the end of the day.

Heather packs up the car as efficiently as she could. Cold compresses in case of a break in the cast. Additional visors in case it got way too sunny. Assorted vitamin and mineral packs in case I accidentally pass out. I had put $3,000 into air filters and premium air conditioning. That's the one thing with old cars nowadays. All the old filtration systems used to help the highways smell a little bit better and reduce the temperature twenty, maybe thirty degrees. Yet the increase of foreign particles in the air has rendered them essentially useless, much less the fifty-degree oscillation between acceptable air temperatures and the outside. The R8 is great that way – it may burn gas like a truck climbing the Rockies but its tight, sexy body keeps you cool and looking cool. Getting my immovable frame into the car took some work. We lever my leg into the spot and gently shifted the rest of my body into the car. It's a tight fit.

About twenty minutes later, Murph shows up. The sun reflected off his teeth as he stepped out the car door.

He looks confused. Maybe it's the fact that Heather really is gorgeous. You put a girl of that caliber behind the wheel of a car with this much sex appeal and it can be overwhelming for most men. Maybe he hadn't seen me with a different woman in decades. I hadn't either.

"You still don't look so hot, chump." He rested his arm on top of the car and stared into the window. Concern dripped off his face, one bead of sweat at a time.

"I know. I'm trying to bounce back fast. Work never sleeps."

"You gotta sleep." He pushed down his sunglasses and looked across the center console to Heather. "He's sleeping, right?"

"Of course. I knock him out each night." She tossed her hair breezily.

"Nyquil or hammer?"

"Baseball bat." She grinned.

"Right answer. That's what Pops recommended." He smiles, reaches into his pocket, revealing a little box. "Attach this right behind the rear-view mirror. The sensor will pick it up from about half a mile away so you shouldn't have any problems getting on the A highway. If you do, highway patrol will catch you before you get on. *Kindly* explain that you had to swap out cars."

He stuffs his hand into his other pocket to display a plastic strip. "Heather, Roger was right. You kinda do look like my wife. Put this on your left arm under your sleeve just in case you get pulled over or get scanned. I have a new code that will basically let you be ID'ed as my wife for all of forty-five seconds. Even the cop's visors will think you're her. It'll work, trust me. I didn't have to fudge the numbers too much." He winked. "You two lovebirds better hit the road. If you want to get there while it's still open, that is."

"Thanks again, Murph. I'll hit you back this week, drinks or something."

"No drinks, dude, not for a while."

"That's right, Roger, you can't be boozing until the medicine passes through your system," Heather scolded.

"Right, right. Well, I'll hit you back."

"Of course, bub. Have a safe trip."

"You too," I offer. He turns around to get back in the car. Heather revs the engine a few times and smiles. Power like this shoulda been illegal back then, like it is now. No matter.

We pass through downtown in a matter of minutes. The A branch of Highway 5 begins around City of Commerce. We get into the far left lane and hit the logjam of traffic. My car is clearly the oldest. I lock the doors... really a pointless move, but it makes me feel better. On either side, a smattering of Korean and American cars, clearly not intended for the 5A lane, inch forward slowly, combating their neighbors for the next few feet of space. The car temperature rises as we idle in the hot sun. This old combustion engine has always been a bit more unstable since the emergence of the nucloud several years ago. The engineers I grew up with never expected temperatures like this, let alone that a car would run for several hours in it.

The California Highway Patrol begins its ritual fly-through to inspect 5A. First they clear the stagnant expressway by moving cars to either side. Too many cars funnel into too few lanes, even more cars trying to sneak in illegally. The 5A is only a few years old, built out of necessity to speed through the now-ruinous, dangerous sections of Orange County. The ruins cannot be summed up as the result of economic failure, environmental disaster, or even the roving "conglomerates" that pillaged whole regions of Southern California into rubble. This reality, of "free"-ways, had devolved into parking lots for opportunistic gangs and looters. That meant the A-passes sold out several hours after they were announced, bought either for efficiency or fear for life. Forgeries can be bought up and down the state and they don't do the trick.

Highway 5 always had its sketchy sections while we were growing up. A twenty mile trip could show how the highway could lay waste to whole communities by sheer proximity. Now, 5A keeps you away from that. In theory. Several hundred feet in the air, the lucky few on 5A have the privilege to observe the chaos below them, zipping along as fast as possible to escape the rancorous fights in the concrete jungle below.

The slight pitter-patter of rain hitting the car means only one thing: the highway patrol is above us. It's customary for the CHP to check all automobiles and their passengers who tried to use 5A. A few drops of water trickle down from above, coating the edges of the car, and all of the sudden the automobile's inners are illuminated, from the engine to baby in a mother's belly. The heat wave scan rustled through and Heather gets visibly nervous. I figure we would have little to worry about. Today she is Jane Murphy, my friends' wife.

The highway patrol hovers above us for several seconds. I turn down the music to hear what was happening. A palpable low whirl filled the air, all speedy and slow. The car rattles slowly, then began to wobble back and forth.

"This isn't good." Heather closes her eyes and clutches on to the door handle, white-knuckling the damn thing. I begin to laugh.

"Why are you laughing?" She shoots her eyes at me. I can't stop though. This is too funny. "Roger, this really doesn't help. Why are you laughing? I can't keep my hands on the steering wheel!" I lose my concentration, my eyes vibrating inside their cavities, the skin on my hands unable to maintain a firm grip. Then it stops. An unknown person knocks on my window.

"Don't roll it down, Roger."

"I think I have to." I lower the window a few inches. A patrol officer had dropped down from the hovering ship above. The worst part about the new masks and visors they wear is that you couldn't see their eyes or mouth. I can't tell if he is happy or sad, the plastic blocking all human emotion. His gloved hands clench, the taser and the pacifier ready to fire.

"Hello, officer." I weakly smile. The sun spills in, a white sheen of temporary blindness.

"Hello, sir. Is this car registered for Highway 5 dash A?" The sonic enhancer gives his voice a low rumble, echoing off the titanium body of the car.

"No, but I had to borrow the driver for the day. Mrs. Jane Murphy over here volunteered to help drive me down."

"We have already scanned the car, Mr. Escobar. Mrs. Murphy is allowed to drive. For safety concerns, we do not want any breakdowns on the A lane. It's been more dangerous than usual the past few days." He bent down and peered inside. "And a frail man as yourself would be eaten alive out there. Let alone Mrs. Murphy."

"Sir, I've worked with the city of Los Angeles for the past decade. I've had this car longer. We've had work done on it to safety specs. The brakes are air-locked, the air filtration system is only a few years old, and the tires are an alloy the DWP had approved for cars built before 2015. To be quite frank...," I shove down my glasses, "I think your visors and gear might need more updating. They need to up your budget, you know."

He laughs. The car shakes with his low, bassy grumble. "They do. Maybe you can help us get that." He gazes at his tablet, then the car, and then leans back down. "You'll be fine once you get on the A-5. The ship will clear the road – most of the cars ahead of you are there illegally. When you see the first car move just follow the path."

"Thanks, officer."

"Thank you. Enjoy your drive." He presses a few buttons on the tablet, stands rigid, and crosses his arms. The ship emits a long, high-frequency sound and the officer begins to rise up into the sky.

Heather releases her grip on the door handle. "How did you do that?"

"Lawyer card. Officers always think I know someone when I use big words. Pay attention to the road."

I point at the cars in front of her while the low rumble hits the seat of my pants. The R8 and the ground shake violently. The GM roadster ahead of us shifts to the left, almost crushing itself into the center divider. Heather places her hands on the wheel, carefully navigating us through this subtle channel provided by the CHP. Car after car moves to the left or the right, a forced passageway created by the sonic pulse. We reach the 5A and, with nary a hitch, hit 130 miles an hour. I close my eyes, see Adrianna in a ball gown ready to dance, and forget that I was going anywhere.

CHAPTER

The best thing about the injury is the excuse. Other than the meeting in San Diego, it has been a sort of paradise. Due to San Diego, I avoided the Wednesday night escapades at the Roosevelt Hotel's Spare Room with the classic doctor's note excuse. I wanted to go to the birthday party, I really did. But I'd have problems with the stairs. Thursday, my monthly event at the L.A. Scotch Society, was basically worthless since Doc didn't want me to have any liquid that could thin my blood. That meant no scotch. I put Murph and Jane on the list for me. They would enjoy a sixteen-year bourbon more than me. Or at least put it to better use.

Work had sorted itself out pretty well other than Romero. Most clients settled at prearranged amounts. All we had to do was wait for payment. Those that didn't were sent forms for arbitration proceedings, mediator selection, what have you, and are billed at the normal rate. I know this sounds like a whole bunch of a fancy talk. But the long and the short of it is that I got to bill out my hours while socialized medicine took care of me. Working shouldn't be this easy. It should be illegal.

Now, a frantic battle to get healthy enough for the weekend. Scar tissue hasn't developed and this morning I could use my leg, at least, in the most minor of twitches, stretches, and extensions. I figure if I could gather the strength to use a cane I won't have to cancel my Friday appointments. I have to show up at the bank to verify all the settlement money in the client bank account. Next is a lunch with Jules, which I really don't want to do, to take the deed to the condo. Then back to the office to deal with the leftover paperwork from Wednesday to verify Romero's status as a naturalized citizen without any cartel influence. Finally, after all that bullshit, a good night's sleep at T.D.S. And, if I I am lucky, a trip to the boat.

Today's rehab should be really fun. A lot of massage and muscle relaxation, the old-fashioned way. The primary bleeding has ended and my scabs shrunk to, well, acceptable levels. Heather did a great job on the stretches and the yoga-like workout was great for my heart rate this morning. I feel more limber than ever, the leg flexible and regaining strength. I can walk about fifteen feet unassisted, thirty or so on the cane. My final major test? To lift a heavy weight with the leg. So far, I can handle about seventy pounds on old lefty.

"We need you at a hundred pounds before I can clear you for normal activity," Heather instructs.

"Seventy today means a hundred tomorrow, boss," I say.

"No, Roger."

"Yes, Heather. You know I have mutant healing powers. I mean look at my hair," exceptionally unkempt and thrown into fuzzy, curly mohawks, "and this awesome beard," miraculously full and wolf-like after a week without a shave. "It's so ON. Give me the yellow-and-blue suit, I might as well be Wolverine."

She laughs. "What about the adamantium bones?"

"You've seen what's in my pants. It's ON." I grinned.

"Cool the jets, ya ham," she says, tousling my hair. "This is official. I can't leave you until you meet the basic, minimal competencies for a seven-year-old. And you aren't doing yourself any favors since we went to San Diego yesterday."

"I know. I'll put in double time tonight. How can we make this go faster?"

"Well... I guess by not putting in double time. If you sleep all, and I mean ALL, night, no alcohol or sleeping aids, your body is going to naturally regenerate the tissue faster. You know how athletes take days off? It's like that. A little rest, regeneration, and maybe tomorrow morning I can clear your sorry ass."

"I guess I can't play soccer on Sunday, then?"

"Not unless you want to risk never playing soccer again. Idiot." Heather has figured out that, for me, tough love is the best love.

"Alright. So what's for dinner?"

"Well, you have about eighty bucks left on your meal budget for the week. Let's go big. You need heavy proteins and carbs to regenerate that tissue. Maybe put some fat on you, you scrawny worm. How about a twelve-ounce steak, some polenta, a few fried brussels sprouts, and a glass of Chianti?"

"I can have a glass of wine? Are you Italian? My dream girlfriend is Italian. At least I think she's Italian. That meal sounds as Italian as a Fiat in the repair shop."

"Consider the wine a treat. And no, I'm not Italian. But I drive a Fiat."

"Oh," I say. She strolls the room. I blindly stare at the video screen. Did I offend her? I am about to watch *Hoop Dreams,* really unsure whether I need to go file some papers or just watch the movie for the fifth or sixth time in my life. I decide to just watch some mindless TV for a few minutes. I don't mean to offend someone who was so nice to me. I guess that's my bad habit.

The meal is wonderful. I ask her if she wants to watch a movie with me. She agrees. We eat in near silence, eyes transfixed on *Hoop Dreams*. She has never seen it before. Nineteen ninety-one was definitely before she was born. She asks questions about life back then. I don't know much; I was young. Inner-city Chicago might be more dangerous now, with better guns and worse police, but we are both shocked to see how much the world really hasn't changed. The city is still a jungle, minorities are still underrepresented in politics, and a cycle of poor education and drugs lets the street govern themselves. Heather looks engrossed. So am I.

The movie ends late enough to call it an evening. By my estimate I can get eight, nine hours of comfortable sleep. We elevate the leg and put cold compresses around it. She tucks me into bed. No dreams follow. I snooze, content, a food coma rocking me gently to sleep.

We start earlier than I expect. At 8 a.m. in the morning the stretching feels vicious. After a brutal amount of calisthenics she makes me balance on my bad leg. That's tough enough. By the time I have to lift the weights I am exhausted. Seventy pounds is ok. Eighty is tougher. Eighty-five pretty rough. And ninety is pure stress, a difficult test on this already weak and difficult leg. Like it wasn't insulting enough that this primitive lifting exercise is my test. A grown-ass man, forced to do stupid, menial tasks...

"Quit complaining, Roger. And lift. Focus," she instructs.

I try. Over and over again. I max out at eighty-five pounds. To lift ninety pounds feels impossible. But nothing is impossible until you say it is. So I try and try until I don't know what trying feels like anymore. My leg becomes a rusty sewer grate, stuck because I am too weak to push through the parts that had oxidized together.

"I don't think I can do it," I say.

"Yes, you can." She straightens my leg, stacks the weights one by one, and stares down at me. "Let's do it this way."

"Which way?"

"I'll apply ten pounds of pressure with my hand if you can handle the other ninety. After all, I know you don't like being held down by a woman, do you?"

"Not really." I lower the ninety pounds down slowly. She applies her weight at the final section of the descent. My knees crank into my chest. As I push up, as hard as I possibly can, the weight subsides. She grins at me, both hands in the air. "See, you can do it."

"Does that count?"

"In my book. Now let me cook some breakfast and we can both get out of here." She shuffles to the kitchen. In a few minutes I receive a Denver omelette and a shot of espresso. I get a reward even when I quit before the finish line. So I shave, shower and dress, careful around the bandages, and position a compress around the leg to keep my gait decent. Now I can accomplish everything I need to for the day. Like I want to. Like Heather wants me to. She gathers her gear and clothing, preparing to leave.

"Roger, just wondering... How do you feel when you walk out of T.D.S.?"

"Pretty good. How did you know I go there?"

"Your bills."

"OK... why are you asking?"

"Just out of curiosity. Next time you go there, maybe you should check the food they give you and test your blood."

"For what?"

"I've heard that they might be doping. But not steroids. You know, we nurses got our own web boards too."

"Thanks for the warning."

First, to the bank. Mary, my account manager, notices the hobble. She thinks my cane was a blackjack or some other prison weapon. She may be joking. We go through the normal procedures. Each deposit verifies against my ledger, all discrepancies receive validation, partial payments are reclassified as incomplete payments in part. A mundane process, an almost exclusive action for bureaucratic purposes. At this branch the coffee was good, so my few moments there were not in vain. When I mean good, I mean not just reconstituted cups of coffee flavor. They brew on the spot. A true rarity. Nobody has time for that.

FOREIGN WATERS

We finish at 11:30. Lunch with Julia was at 12:15, across town in a suburban section of the northern valleys that I hadn't seen in three years. Near her parents' old place.

I arrive there ten minutes early, parking halfway down the street. When I walk up to the most chichi-la-la sandwich shop in the neighborhood, she is already there, thumbs dancing up and down her phone, engaged in some conversation. She looks good, sun-kissed, and freckles pop over her tanned chest. The natural, trademark nervous shifts reveal fresh tan-lines across the bra strap. The good life is pretty good.

"Looking good, Jules." I give a toothy grin.

"Dapper as always, Roger. Where did you park?"

"Over there. I always liked walking down that street." I sit in the rickety metal chair and squeeze my hands on the compress. The pain sears into my bones – there will be hell to pay for this. Maybe a scar now. Hopefully not a limp, just to escape her seeing the car again. It'll take a stronger wound to stop an honest man like me – it'll take a lie.

"What's wrong?" She turns her nose in and frowns at me.

"Nothing. Just a little weak today."

"You're wearing a jacket in this heat. Are you sick? You look paler than normal, you sorry excuse for a Hispanic." Casual racism is our thing.

"I'm not a Hispanic – I'm American, whatever you want to call me. And yes, I've had a cold for a few days, so it was a great excuse to put on this old jacket." I open up the Barbour Rook jacket to reveal the lining and new stitch details. Two weeks ago Armand relined it with a blue pattern, grey seals with fuzzy noses balancing balls every inch and a quarter in every direction. "You got this for me when we first visited London. I just had to make some repairs from too much wear."

"It still fits! But don't change the subject, Roger, you were favoring your right leg. Did you injure old lefty in soccer again?"

"Sure."

"Yeah, you always did swing to the left." She pulls down her sunglasses and winks. She loves a good dirty joke as much as I do. "Remember when you got raked down your shin guards scoring that goal? That was so gross."

"Nowhere as gross as watching it. To think, if you went to that game you coulda seen how metal spikes can't stop me."

"Eww. But you scored."

"Hell yeah. You know me. Scoring is my thing." And I gave her a similar stare down and wink. She looks disgusted. Too disgusted to play along. "Be glad you never went to the games."

"So how did you hurt it?"

"Soccer."

"For a lawyer, you're a terrible liar."

"For a banker, you care too much." We both laugh, a joke older than our marriage. The small talk became pretty small. We dance around the points we really wanted to talk about. I order a sandwich and she got a salad. Lunch evolves into a formal proceeding. In law it has a fancy name, but really, it's just giving me the damn deed. We joked about college for a while and made fun of the clothes we used to own. Thank God most of the photos exist in hard copy only. I considered scanning all the photos to create a digital record to share with all my friends. But the shoebox that held those four hundred photos rests under the gun in the closet to collect dust. Impossible to remove, forget, or replace.

"Daddy wants to know you'll take care of it."

"It isn't some man cave, Julia. Besides, I bought flowers a few days ago."

"What??? Like, living ones?"

"Real, live flowers. Smelled like roses too."

"Boy, you're all grown up. Next thing you'll tell me is that you got rid of the sports car for some dad van."

"Well, I did just buy a new Cadillac."

"All you boys. You all need your toys." She slaps the deed into my hand and judges me under a long gaze. Then the smile of approval. The physical manifestation of a great conclusion in her head to validate about any and all circumstances between us.

"And now I have another one. Thanks. I'm glad we got this out of the way."

"Me too, Roger. Do you want to eat?" She pointed at the food. Her salad certainly wasn't any colder, but I hadn't touched the sandwich. Strange.

"When do I not want to eat?"

"When it's healthy, ya goob. Deep fried butter is more your style. You haven't changed your diet since our first date."

"Yeah, but let's be honest – heavy beers and a hearty burger is the key to your heart too."

"Was. I can't eat that way anymore."

"It shows." She twitches as I say that. "Wait. I didn't mean it that way. I mean that you look good, healthier. Not anything else."

"Yeah. OK. Whatever you say."

"Come on, Julia, it was just a compliment that I messed up. You know I didn't mean it that way."

"Maybe not towards me. But at me? Come on, Roger."

"Seriously. I got nothing to lie about here."

"I know you don't. You have nothing, really. Except this." She pointed at the deed. "And some old cars."

"I like my old cars."

"All you boys." She snorts. Her hands cross over her chest and her focus seems to be on the roof of the store across the street. Christ. This isn't good.

"Yeah... I guess." I tried to focus on whatever she was looking at. "Yeah..."

"You don't have to say anything." She straightens her head and her sunglasses point nowhere, her obvious line of vision beneath them. This is dangerous. Her instability always grew in her moments of calm introspection, her eyes unfocus so as to focus her mind on my every word.

"So..."

"It's OK, Roger. You can leave if you want."

"But I do want to eat."

"Honestly, I probably won't. So if you want to eat alone, by all means..." She steps out of the chair, without a single glance behind her, and walks down the street. Walks past where she said she parked, past the next block, and into the shopping district. By then her silhouette is a mere outline, a bob of hair bouncing across the street until she appears as just another body, a nameless shape unwilling to stop for anything or anyone. I look at my sandwich. It's the same order I made over a decade ago on one of our first dates. Heavy on the horseradish, thinly sliced roast beef, a blend of lettuces, and a few slices of tomato.

It never looked so disgusting.

I place fifty dollars underneath my cup of iced tea, grab my cane, and hobble to my feet. The deed sits comfortably in my jacket's chest pocket. The condo finally mine, after all these years. But I could care less. Downtown is the next destination and, thankfully, Julia is gone. Extra time, so no need to rush.

CHAPTER

T he drive is easier than I expect. Going in the opposite direction of traffic has benefits. Heather had given me temporary handicapped parking so it was much easier to get into the office. No more parking on the eighth floor only to switch elevators to take me up to thirty-five. I grab my briefcase from the back of the car and slowly lug it behind me through the lot. All of Romero's paperwork is in here and, with C.B.P. agents arriving in under an hour, I want to get at least a little bit prepared.

The office smells stale, like the coffee hadn't been changed for a few days or the bananas had begun to turn. I forgot referral mode didn't activate the rest of the office. Oops.

But a few touches to the identifier box brings Dorothy back to life and with her the whole office. Her screen flickers a few times, the nondescript black cube hums and leaks heat. With a wave of my hand, light blue dots extends from the top of the box in a large semicircle, a slow coagulation of particles above it. Her three-dimensional form radiates into place. Dorothy's physical incarnation is basically Tinkerbell in jeans and a blazer, casual and innocent enough to not scare away the simpler clients. If she was too high tech it would keep away the people who couldn't afford lawyers. They all thought that they would pay for her. And they do, really. But it all depends on what work they need and theirs don't fund the modern touches to the office. That said, she classes up the place. I made sure she did.

"Good to see you again, sir." After twenty years of avatar evolution, with Dorothy as a high-end example, the programmers still haven't made a perfect smile.

"Thanks, Dorothy. Please deactivate your referral mode. I'll be in the office today and next week should be back to normal."

"Of course. We've missed you here." She points into the particle field and made a "come here!" motion with a frantic wave of her little arms. A bunch of folders slowly fell out, each of the case names morph into photos, and then body scans, of each respective client. Jordan Chandler's heavy shoulders offered a massive paw in the air. That little kid Seth Collins jumps and waves, his chest surgery scars displayed prominently like the image we received ten days ago. Dorothy tries to show her teeth at me. "Where do you want to begin?"

"Well, please give me the turnover for the past three days."

"Monday had fifteen potential clients come in but due to the circumstances beyond our control and a lack of automation, as referral mode was not on, those fifteen were shown the door. When you activated the script on Tuesday, we looked at and accepted nine clients. They were sent to three different firms: Reina, Kessel, and Villar. We gained $4,421.50 at the loss of $1,222 that day, to include rent and appropriate expenses."

"OK, the detail is great. But I just want the numbers right now."

"Certainly. Wednesday was a profit of $2,125.22, Thursday was uncommonly slow and we lost $244.12. Today we have been up $924, up until you switched modes a few minutes ago."

"Fantastic. Can you please have all the new cases organized alphabetically and put in a folder for me? I want to check them after this meeting."

"Certainly. May I ask what meeting we have today?"

"Did I send you the updates on Romero? My nurse was supposed to upload the updates when we returned from San Diego."

"No, sir. I received two updates, one on Tuesday and one this morning, both not from you."

"Please recite the updates."

"Of course. Transmission received from C.B.P., San Diego County. Cruz Romero has been detained at the Otay Border Surveillance Station. Entry into the United States through John Wayne Airport, Long Beach, California, denied. Assets frozen upon entry. Request for legal counsel received at 13:26 via collect call. Accepted. Would you like to hear Romero's verbal request?"

"No. Is there more?"

"Yes. Transmission received this morning to request additional verification documentation and a notice that the C.B.P. will distribute a file docket to me on Monday."

"A file docket?"

"Yes, sir. It will include a case history and a notice of release."

"What? Release of what?"

"I was not given a copy of the release. But if I had to guess..."

"Dorothy, we know you don't guess very well."

"But if I did, it would be the affirmative release of all claims against the client Romero." She snaps her fingers, cocks her head, and the avatar of Romero lumbers forward, a few backpacks slung over his shoulder, paper falling out with each step. Her hand disappears into the backpack, pulls out a folder, and points to the final slot in it. Her system has already partitioned that section to close the case. The case is closed?

"So..."

"We just have to wait. Can you please tell me about the meeting you have scheduled? I will need to get coffee ready. And get some fresh air in here, I know clients hate that!" She flutters off the viewing platform for a few seconds to take care of... something. Who knows.

"You're sure that a notice of release is coming?"

"Yes, sir."

"Let's check what's in my bags then." I lift the satchel to place it on the desk.

"Are you in pain, sir?"

"Not really. It's just more numb than anything. This week has been pretty rough."

"I can only imagine."

"Yes, yes you can." I unlock the top, dumping out the contents. Papers pile on top of each other and eventually off the table. She moves off the platform to hover over the loose sheets and quickly scan the contents. Like an information-sucking hummingbird twittering from nectar to nectar, flower to flower to flower to flower. I mess up the papers as much as I can. Otherwise she'll have to call in some noisy machines to do that for her. "I haven't looked at these since before I drove down on Wednesday, Dorothy. Any idea what these are, besides my scattered notes?"

"I appreciate the mess but I will need some more time. From my initial scans it seems that you have..." She does a back flip, shakes her head, and points at each sheet of paper respectively. "Umm, you have several pages of documents from Mr. Scheffler, Esq., as to negotiation tactics with the officials you met with. These over here are Romero's trust files and bank deposits for the branch of First World Trust, Peoria, Illinois. And finally, the binder you have dumped out has the signatures of Ignacio Martinez, C.B.P. operations manager, on a sheet to confirm Romero's status as a legal entrant to the country. This paper...," she flutters on top of a sheet and sniffs it, "has four signatures from Phillip Graziano, Thomas Kerry, Lucas Benaglia, and John Richter, all C.B.P. holding officers. This released them from further claims against Romero and future lawsuits for any maltreatment of him."

"What?" What?!?!

"Would you like me to repeat that?"

"No, Dorothy. I'm just in shock."

"But you were there, sir. See, your signature is right here. And here and here and here. It's everywhere. Although it is uncommonly sloppy. You like to use a more stylized G for your middle initial, and the R at the end generally has a sharp turn, not a heavy pen dragging off the page."

"Yeah. Yeah, I know. I just..."

"What, sir?"

"I really don't remember. Can you get my nurse Heather on the line? She gave me her portable number. Should be able to reach her now. Also, can you call me Mr. Escobar for the rest of the day? Sir feels too formal and I want to feel normal." I flick her card onto the table and begin to remove my jacket.

"Of course, Mr. Escobar. I'll call her right now." I get comfortable in my chair, rearrange the screens and tablets, and smooth down my hair.

"Hey, Roger." Heather's sweetness comes through the speaker loud and clear.

"Hey, Heather. Just want to let you know I've been moving pretty well. I got some pain around my thigh but it ain't so bad. You did a great job. I'll send your boss some glowing comments and the likes."

"Thanks, Roger. That's kind of you."

"Of course. Listen. I need to know what happened when we got down to San Diego. The last thing I remember was when the cars were cleared out. I think I remember stepping out of the car. But I'm not sure."

"You don't remember anything?"

"Nothing. I remember how hot it was in the car on the way down, that's about it."

"OK. I had a feeling you'd ask about this."

"Why?"

"First things first: you stopped talking shortly after the trip. I thought you were just exhausted from the day so I let you sleep. You were lightly humming, not quite snoring. It was kinda cute. So when I drove the car down to San Diego I thought nothing of it. When we got there..."

"Yeah?"

"When we got there, Roger, you looked unchanged. We only had about ten minutes to get you out of the car. You weren't moving. I gave you a shot of adrenaline, which seemed to wake you up, but it was like you were in a trance. Your eyes didn't focus, your heart rate went up, but you were like a dead weight. I had a guard help me lift you. He was a nice guy and I gave him a story that made you sound like the great, crippled genius of lawyers. We got you into the wheelchair and I noticed you still weren't reacting properly to the adrenaline. So I gave you an animatizer."

Those are a bit dangerous. Animatizers have been used in my profession to draw information out of people unable to convey their thoughts. More specifically, anyone with severe head trauma, stuck in a coma, or in a vegetative state. With the right cues, the animated patient can answer questions, ask relevant ones, and even give commands for objects it wants or needs. They have a tendency to backfire into one's subconscious. Anything from the patient's last sexual experience to a favorite toy as a child can weave itself into the conversation.

"OK, I get that. But how did you get me to keep on topic? This wasn't easy stuff, ya know?"

"You were kinda on autopilot. It was pretty funny, but it worked."

"You're saying I... um... functioned... worked, acted lifelike? Not like a reanimated corpse?"

"You were fine. I just whispered into your ear what you needed to hear to help guide you. I was prepared for this."

"Prepared?"

"Come on, Roger, I'm a nurse. I have your whole medical history faster than," she snaps her fingers four times in a row, "and change."

"Wait. So the animatizer..."

"Was something we prepared for." What the hell does that even mean?

"Prepared for?"

"Come on, Roger, this isn't rocket science. You of all people." A sympathetic look melts from her eyes, like a sister catching her brother joyriding dad's car. I feel like a child.

"Umm... that I'm sick?"

"You could put it that way. You've been going to T.D.S. too much." I shot her a blank look. It didn't click. "Roger. It takes... a lot of drugs to sedate someone but keep their imagination active for eight hours. And you've gone there forty-five times in the past twenty weeks."

"How did you know that?"

"It's all in your medical files. Your body has retained significant doses of alprozam, scopolamine, 5-methoxy-diisopropyltryptamine, and some opiate and amphetamine derivatives. When you got checked into the hospital on Sunday, your blood work was transparent. Your body has been trained to accept the drug cocktail as a substitute for sleep. Eventually it will reject it, and when that happens, an animatizer is a way to keep you mentally intact."

"How many times did you say I went to T.D.S.?"

"Forty-five."

"I only remember nineteen." I really didn't have anything left to say; it makes too much sense now. It gets very quiet. I hold my head in my hands and rubs my sore left leg.

"When do you go back?"

"Tonight."

CHAPTER

Dorothy's best attribute is her ability to eavesdrop. Most of my clients never notice. When I sign them up with a quick flip through close to fifty pages of absurd agreements, they never seem to see the clause that every bit of their conversations with me will be overheard by the gadgets placed in this room.. Dorothy, or specifically, this model of her, never transcribes the conversations until I initiate the prompt to do so. But that does not mean that her temporary memory banks aren't always active. A clever way to keep information without actually, as they say, recording. And after the consultation, no matter how long it is, she can recall specific moments in the conversation that were more emotional or had significance. As great as I am at reading my customers, she seems to be better.

I guess I'm not very good if a digital pixie understands human emotion better than me. To no surprise, the second best thing about Dorothy is the cup of green tea she delicately shoved across the table mid-conversation. I needed to hydrate. I hadn't drank water all day, at least as far as I could remember.

It takes a minute or two for me to begin to breathe. Heather stares through the time it took me to regain my breath and sip some tea. Instantly my nasal passages clear and the headache began to recede.

"I've been dehydrated for weeks, haven't I?"

"Yup. You've been operating on fumes. Literally. Whatever water you have gotten has been from ice cubes, soup, what have you. But not directly.

"And you found that out from my medicals."

"Yeah."

"I love you. No really. I do." We aren't in love, I've never kissed her, I've never held her hand. But right now Heather knows me better than I know myself.

"No, you don't."

"OK, you're right. But let me at least have a crush for this day. I didn't know any of this."

"OK."

"But seriously, Heather. Why didn't you tell me this earlier? All you said was that they might be doping."

She furrows her brow and reaches off screen. She waves a stack of papers, blocking the screen. "This is why. The contract you signed when leaving the hospital. I can't do anything that would allow you to possibly endanger yourself. You do that enough on your own. If I told you, 'Roger, you're being drugged,' you would want some semblance of vengeance. It's my job to get you healthy enough for me to leave. Nothing more, nothing less. And right now you might be the healthiest you have been in two years. No smoking, no heavy drinking for a week, plenty of rest, and a low amount of drug addiction. By modern standards, of course."

"Of course. I guess I should be thanking you then. The past few days were really great for me." I smile weakly.

"They were great for me too, Roger. But now that you're well, it's time for you to do the rest of the work."

"I'm with you. You know just because I understand 'the law,'" as I throw my quotation fingers at the screen, "doesn't mean I can understand everything. Health is one of them. And that's just cause I'm lazy."

"Or sad." Her eyes looked darker when she said this, the pupils radiating outwards.

"Probably."

"Yup. Probably."

"While all this talk about my mental health is great, I gotta be honest. I don't remember any of this. Was I hallucinating, stuck in sleep paralysis, or both? My bank account hasn't shown that I've been gone to T.D.S. forty-five times."

"You're getting back billed. The charges are adding up but you only pay for one visit a week, not two. Eventually you'll have to pay it up." She looks a bit bored. She chews on strands of her hair.

"So like a personal trainer showing up unannounced."

"You could say that."

"Will I be OK tonight?"

"Are you going to go?"

"Well, I signed up. I've been looking forward to this date all week. Come on, Heather, you've seen my robust social life. Girls are tripping over themselves to be bored to death while having dinner with me."

"OK, that was actually funny."

"Thanks. But seriously."

"You'll be fine. Like I said, you've grown a healthy resistance to this drug cocktail. It replaced a sleep cycle more than once a week. I'd hate to say you're dependent upon it, but these are all serious drugs. The combination alone should be dangerous. But I wouldn't be surprised if it was more dangerous to quit."

"Quitting is for losers."

"Dead losers." Yup.

"You said it's not steroids. And to pay attention to the food when I get in there. Any ideas on what to do?"

"Well consider this. The patient intake form from Sunday evening reflect the effects forty-eight hours after your initial dose. It might be easier for you to quit, if you want to, by finding some samples to test how heavily you have been sedated. I'm sure you can figure out a way to test them."

"I'm not sure if I want to quit."

"So don't. Look... Roger, you asked for my help. Can't you let me help you?" She has a point. I don't necessarily agree with it, I mean, I don't need much help right now. The divorce finalized years ago, business is up, the condo is now mine. I feel better than I ever have, my dreams are better than they've ever been.

"OK. I'll see what I can do. But I have to go tonight. There's a lot on the line. I've been trying to figure out who this girl is for months now. She's beautiful."

"But Roger..." She sniffs, pulls her flowery, full blouse above her nose, faces down and gazes with possible tears welling up in her eyes. "I thought you said you loved me."

"Oh, I always will. I've chased this other ghost for months now, maybe more than I ever realized. Hey... were you an actor before a nurse?"

"How'd you know?"

"This is Los Angeles, you know."

"Bye, Roger."

"Bye, Heather. Talk soon."

"Sure, whatever." The tablet clicks off. I exhale and collapse into the chair.

"Dorothy, can I get some music? Something light-hearted?"

"Sure thing, Mr. Escobar. I've waited all day to play music! Would you like anything to eat?"

"Not especially. Can you get me a few syringes please?"

"Of course, Mr. Escobar. Whatever you want."

"Maybe I should fall in love with you, Dorothy." The pixie giggles, twirls in circles, and spins into a few back flips.

"Oh, that would be lovely, but I don't think he would be happy."

"He?"

Well. I've been seeing someone too..." She scampers off of the platform. Her little grunts and whispered conversation could only mean she is convincing someone to reveal them self. After several seconds she appears, dragging Romero by the hand. I laugh.

"Oh, really?"

"He's really great! He's so strong! He carries all this stuff, never complains, and when we talk, it's so simple! He doesn't ask me to do anything!" She floats above and lounges on his back. Romero's expression didn't really change. I don't think I patched the case files to have emotional responses. I get enough of those already from the clients.

"That's great, dear. I give you my blessings."

"Thanks! You are the best boss ever! Let me get you what you asked for. And here's some music." A little blue record player appears next to her and she places the needle on the record. A track from the mid-nineties. I can't remember the name of the song, but the melody I can't forget. Perfect.

My mail slot jiggles under the weight of a small white box. Care of Query Diagnostics. We've been in business together for a while and these are some special ones that they have given me in the past. I haven't used them, of course. But when a client comes in, concerned about some product he ate or a bad pill, this is the fastest way to find out what it is. The blood is drawn painlessly when attached to any visible blood vessel. It fills up in under a second. And I can put it back in the mail slot, punch in the mailing code, and Query will receive it in under five minutes. I'll get the results in an hour or two. Being in the same building certainly helps.

To test the food and drink means I will have to be clever. Blood tests are simple. I can always slip a syringe into my sleeve, hide one in a breast pocket, or even under the sole of my shoe. It may seem a bit obvious and it probably is. But food samples are another deal.

"Dorothy, where can I get glass vials?"

"One second, Mr. Escobar. Query has two-inch-long vials, about half an inch thick, for only $20 per vial. I can get three-inch vials for $30, et cetera."

"I need one of those. Place the order. But I might have... leftovers from dinner. I need something small, easy to carry, and I won't need a bag. Tupperware won't work. Maybe a plastic box with a removable lid, something about two by two by two?"

"Do you mean inches?"

"Yes."

"I can get that from another provider. It'll take a few hours."

"I have to leave the office by six. I got two hours."

"If I can make them deliver it by five-thirty, is that acceptable?"

"Of course."

"Well then, Mr. Escobar, please just relax, listen to the music, and wait for your orders to come in! And do drink that tea. You don't want to make Heather mad. Do you really love her?" Dorothy offers a big smile. In the background a new song begins, the lyrics move in like headlights in the fog of my head, *chop another line like a coda with a curse...*

"I was joking, Dorothy."

"I still can never figure out when you are joking!" She pouts.

"I know. Me neither." I close my eyes for a minute and focus on breathing. The caffeinated rush of the day has begun to wear off. Every sip of tea removed pressure from my sinus cavities. Dehydration was no joke. Heather was right all along. The medications, the drugs, the lack of regular sleep, the alcohol dependency, all seem tied together. I've been at the location more than I realize, possibly in my sleep, possibly against my will, possibly unable to shake the differences between the two. I have two free hours before my appointment. I might want to get some rest beforehand.

CHAPTER

have a special jacket at the office that I never take home. If I took it home when I was married I'm positive her questions would never end. In the modern world it's not very clever. This old, heavy jacket in the style of seventy-odd years ago has secret compartments. Back in centuries past, this type of jacket would be great to hold a weapon. You could sling a single-shot pistol into what looked like a change pocket in the inner breast. A secret fold in the coat lining reveals an access point for your hand to point the barrel and grip the trigger. There are lots of spots to drop sharp objects (sharp side up, of course) and hold them in place. This appears as a natural crease mark in the fabric. With a slight push below each object, the handle becomes easy to grasp. A five-inch blade could hide by your side easily. Maybe a revolver. Or a few chunks of an explosive.

I have never used it that way. Miniaturization is human society's most underrated creation. Cumbersome technology gets reduced to mere slivers of carbon or silicon. A beautiful evolution. This jacket, with so many compartments, could hold four or five computers and several data drives that could carry all the information in the entire solar system times ten. But that would be a waste of the jacket.

FOREIGN WATERS

Regardless of ethical considerations, few things are handier than a record of all conversations. Not between my clients and myself – they have all been transcribed in the office, meticulously so, by Dorothy. No, this is for when I'm "on the road." Whether it's at another lawyer's office to negotiate with a stupid insurance company, or a simple explanation of "medium rare" to the burger flipper downstairs, this jacket is in "on" mode. To record, observe, and keep track of all my vitals. If I can figure out a clever way to spin in a circle, the heat scanner in the lower section of the jacket will read the body temperatures of everyone around me. This is especially good to see if someone is a liar. Behind the lapel sits a microphone with a reverse conal shape to allow it to pick out all the sound outside of my jacket. Basically, you won't hear my heart race or my chest heave in a coughing fit. Inside the flap in the left breast pocket a processor ticks away, a meter displaying whatever information it has received from the scanner and how much room is left on the audio drive.

Contrary to what Julia believes, I don't have the gun to shoot people, animals, clay targets, or her. I use it to intimidate if I have to or as a prop when a client has to "reenact" whatever it was they went through. The gun isn't real to me. Just a prop and occasional security blanket with no place in this jacket. And the gun has no place in my life other than for work. The jacket is the same.

I haven't used the other sections. Yet. They are just empty stretches of fabric that contain air, mothballs, and lint. But they can be rigged in only a few minutes and I'm about to walk out the door. So to get to the next door we'll have to be a bit crafty. The metal detector should be no problem but to avoid the camera, well, that will take a clever movement. I guess I'll have to take some time to find some private parts. Of the place. You know.

Assuming that the jacket can get safely inside the location and rest comfortably in my locker, untouched, there are more important questions to answer. Specifically about her. I've spent the past few weeks learning about her, the girl from who knows where, with an accent from somewhere not here, with a name so familiar and lovely, Adrianna, that it might not even be real. The strategy had been simple for so long: remember what I was supposed to ask her, wait for a right time to ask the question, communicate with visual cues instead of verbal ones in order to avoid suspicion from our highly monitored encounters. The last encounter did not give much of an opportunity to get, well, any real information that I can use to ascertain an identity or location.

Maybe this will take different questions or a different form of questions. The cutoff felt too sudden last time. If I get caught now I will be "banned" or "restricted" for however long and that just means more time away from those answers. The system administrators or monitors, whatever the company uses, will watch more attentively than before and listen to every tidbit of conversation. It'll be curious to find out what they watch, though. Or if there is a way to keep them out.

FOREIGN WATERS

***

The walk is crisp and I can't really explain why I'm walking at this speed but dear Lord is it fun to keep walking at this pace because it just stays so automated to move forward on the one then two then one then two in quick succession because it really isn't a straight walk anymore, more of a run, isn't it...

When you see a fire further down a snowy, wintery path, well, you'd run for it too. Flames leap high and evaporate into the cold of the air. Large enough to engulf low-lying evergreens if the snowfall ever subsides. This must be the reason I run through these woods.

The snow comes down harder now and my boots are somehow impervious to the foot of crushed ice and puddles around each step. I pace in circles because, well, it's fun anyways, but what better to pace around than a woodsy, smelly fire at the crossroads of a white-and-blue forest. The icicles that hang from the trees dangle in an uncommon indigo, imbued by a surreal periwinkle. Everything else feels no different than a classic Northeastern winter, the flowery blue surreal yet tangible.

FOREIGN WATERS

Three paths, always three paths. Few things distinguish them from each other, let alone distinguish the path I came to get here. The path I came from rests one hundred and twenty degrees from the other two. One has a light hazy air, sheets of white light and yellow cutting through the trees. The other trail dramatically shrinks into brush and evergreens after several yards. I really don't know where I am or what decision to make. But to pace like this is still fun so I can just extend this experience as long as I want, after all, I...

I enjoy this fire. A whistle to my left can change all that and it does.

An iron kettle rests five yards away on small bed of coals, on the fringes of the icy glade next to one of the pathways. As much as I want to question how or who put the coals here, or whoever placed such an incendiary delight, the desire remains remote at best. I can hear the percolation of water. The liquid eventually explodes from the iron cell. It's probably been there the whole time I was pacing and I just didn't see it. Dammit.

I try to grab the top handle but, for whatever reason, miss. I grab the lid of the kettle with my bare hands, a smart move when the iron water holder has been heated for several minutes. I can't hold onto the top so I toss it in the forest, water spills everywhere, and examine my fingers. Well, it happened again. I was far too clumsy for my own good and burnt myself. I slowly take one arm out of the jacket and use the fabric as a barrier to shove the kettle off of the small mass of coals. It clatters off and eventually melts its way to the hardened and frozen soil to create a muddy slosh in which to rest. The snow continues to melt upon contact and, theoretically, I could just toss in more snow to evade the loss. But hot water is the commodity here, anything to soothe the heart.

I find the pot and, somehow, three feet further down the hazier pathway, rests a table and a pair of chairs with two cups. The kettle rattles in the self-made snowy enclave and almost refills itself, snow dripping into a steamy interior. I grab it fast. Describing the unfit wood lashed together in a primitive fashion as chairs might be unfair but accurate. I suppose they will be serviceable as they are all I got. I guess it's time for a tea party of one. Again.

I pour half of the pot into my cup and it smells of a roasted essence conjured out of wood I haven't smelled before. The smokiness of the tea, one measly component among its many nuances, starts the voyage of flavor. It rests on a lighter body, an initial odor of orange rind that contains a darker character. A trickery in its reddish hues to reveal a heavy, lustful, strong hint of Ceylon cinnamon. The seat shifts a little bit under me to get far more comfortable, an invitation to contemplate life and the surrounding mysteries, to enjoy the relaxation and clear peace of mind that comes when one stumbles upon a scene of tranquil serenity.

A snowy lump rests on the chair across from me. I reach over and brush the snow off. Once again, another classic from my library;

maybe this translation is a bit different, but while I sit here, reading the book couldn't hurt. *Yet he knew only too well the source of sudden temptation. It was an urge to flee – he fully admitted it, this yearning for freedom, release, oblivion – an urge to flee his work, the humdrum routine of a rigid, cold passionate duty. Granted he loved that duty and even almost loved the enervating daily struggle between his proud, tenacious, much-tested will and growing fatigue, which no one must suspect or the finished product betray by the slightest foundering or neglect...* I close my eyes and begin to breathe through my nose. Here all matter and matters feel rigid and apparent. Life has a tendency to slow down when each breath counts, when the last decision is as important as the next. A work in progress as we try to find environments where we can live forever, and here, I am so fragile, so stuck in this chair. Just another human.

But let's pour one for the person who could not be here. And I take the kettle to the snow-filled cup and begin to pour. Tonight will be long and I will awake with a contemplation of the soul, an offering to all spirits alive and dead for my crimes and infidelities. That cup is for those I wronged, those for whom I have not done my job to the best of my ability, those who I forgot and left behind because I wanted to. Because I spite what I have done and they deserve a drink, even if they are not there. I pull my hood over my head and fan it out, like a cultist waiting his turn.

The snow begins to collect in the cup slower than expected. I guess there remains only so much space in this compact world. I blow some of it off the rim and it falls into the cup with a plop to the bottom. The water has chilled faster than I expect. It must be this wind and those that pass in it, from water particles to sweat to dust from eras that never had people like me. And never will again.

The cup fills with snow.

I sit and dawdle and hold myself to keep warm. I feel cold everywhere. Especially my nose. My ears. My glasses?

My glasses. Somehow unfogged in the cold and the steam. I finally feel them on my face, cold plastic hardening each minute in the tundra.

I hear footsteps behind me and it sounds like what I think it is.

At least what I want it to be.

And I hope it is finally that. I've waited a while to for it to find me.

But I hear a third footstep in an irregular shuffle. Strange things happen in life, but a third leg generally isn't one of them. This thought petrifies me and I can't move for a second. I might appear fully asleep or comatose, a relic from someone else's kill several hours ago. I guess this is a dangerous area as something with three legs walks around here and the only things that I know that do that are...

Something I don't want to see.

So I don't move and I hope it passes. I'm lost to nowhere now. The best thing I can do is be nothing here.

The breath labors and the steps approach me from an acute angle. A purposeful drag of one interaction into one extended engagement. I can see the snout before the body as it drags its nose from side to side to pick up any stray scent. A three-legged dog. A bitch limping, sniffing each crevice of the terrain to find any familiar smell. The poor little girl lost in the forest, tattered, covered by ice and wrapped up in the cold. Wounded from an incident long before me, she adapted an impediment into just another facet of her life and is unafraid of any danger in this environment. The furry coat, unkempt and badly in need of a trim, provides enough warmth to accommodate her movement amid the frozen perils of the terrain.

She dawdles over and I extend my hand. She greets it with a nuzzle. Small teeth and a long thin snout reveal a terrier or possibly a pit-bull mix of some type. She pushes her body against the arm and walks to the fire. I grab the cups and kettle and lever myself out of this oblong recliner chair, somehow more limber than ever before. The coals that the kettle once sat upon still burn so I fill the kettle with snow. I gently nestle the heavy metal contraption upon the tiny furnace of stacked coals. It heats faster than any wave technology that I've ever seen. I kick out the snow to reveal the frozen grass. I place the two cups on the ground and remove my coat. The kettle remains too hot to lift but it works better this way, the coat a natural deterrent for the heat, and I pour the nearly boiling water in the cup with a few chunks of snow to cool it down.

The poor girl drinks the cup dry and wants more. Why she didn't eat snow is beyond me. I'm not very good at biology. Maybe the dog is just dumb. But I pour her glass to the brim and she stares at me with eyes that hit hard and low and into my heart, like she remembers the time that I accidentally left the back door unlocked and she ran into the street unable to contain boundless energy. She bursts out of her physical constraints, unleashed into the street where she was supposed to die but didn't and will never forgive me for that. I still don't know if I know this dog. But I know that look. This is about trust from here on out. So we stare each other down. I lock eyes with the battered and broken only to reveal that we aren't that different. Man and dog have always been friends. Both are social creatures. The relationship remains symbiotic. We demand each other's attention. So she whimpers and nuzzles my knee, the drool needing a little bit attention.

Finally I have someone to drink with.

CHAPTER

A warm nuzzle and push to the left with her body forces me to consider that, yes, it is cold here and to sit quietly keeps us colder. I get down on both knees and rub both her ears gently back and forth. The dog's brow smushes together between her ears and she revels in the attention.

Once again I am presented with a moment of quiet contemplation. I enjoy these moments of silence, so rare and untouchable in my daily routine. In these moments I would rather listen to the wind howl. The ice collects on my nose, the hood of my coat flaps against my face, and I simply observe. One shouldn't explain quiet moments, the overflow of meditative qualities, or frightened, unfocused examinations of one's own character.

One simply must relax and experience.

Quiet is a place. Sometimes to be shared.

Such as with the dog, who is content to sit next to me while I continue to massage her whole body. The pronounced spinal column sticks out, an obvious deficiency from malnourishment, but her body is still warm under the tangled and tussled exterior. Each time I touch the pup's slender body, it gives into my touch. I'm not in this for my own pleasure or let alone to trick it. And the dog senses the sincerity of my emotions, the redemptive qualities of actual, real care. There can be redemption here, not just for me, but for her. Someone cares.

"You're no different no matter where you are, you dear man." For whatever reason I am not startled by another person's voice. Which wouldn't make sense as I was scared shitless when the dog made its slow calculated advance to a far angle of approach. The dog raises its head and ignores my vision to search for the source of the voice. I watch the dog's reaction as the way to gauge my own. She looks from the left and the right and finally finds her focus. Initially the green eyes of the dog flush themselves with overwhelming, unmistakable fear. Within a second the look is gone, acceptance of another person replaces the fright, and the dog returns to gaze lovingly at my face, the man who has accepted her long before the new person.

"Truly. No matter where you are. You are the same." She purrs in the voice that has kept me returning to her for several months now. At this point the conversation feels like mere formality. Yet this is half the fun in this conversation: the formality must be exchanged in order to direct the scene appropriately.

"I don't like change that much."

"I know. But everyone changes, Roger."

"I don't think you will." I stand up, still not facing her, eye contact trained on the seated dog who has found the whole universe in my face.

"I hope I won't, but truly, Roggggggyyyyyerrrrr, I hope you won't." Her hand rests on my shoulder and slowly slides down the length of my back, a calculated and emotive touch that radiates heat wherever the hand wanders. I feel alive and I cannot feel the cold anymore. My body feels engulfed by kinetic forces and energy courses through my body, I cannot repress a smile, I blush, and I forget that I'm supposed to be coy and stick to the song and dance of courtship. My cheeks lock themselves high next to the cheekbones and I put my hand on her hand but don't hold it, just keep it in place, firmly gripped and focused more than ever before in passing the energy I received from her back through her.

We both make attempts to make eye-to-eye contact as I spin around clockwise while she begins to walk around me counterclockwise and we play a small game of hide and seek over my own shoulder until it's clear that she has won, she has won, she has won. And I avoid her eyes but lean in to meet her body and compress our outer layers together, parkas and jackets evolving into larger cushions for the wintertime lover. As I try to move my face into a comfortable place for both of us she pushes her body harder on me and I feel the tightness in her face as she smiles and begins to chuckle. She has won, she has won, she has won. Her leg hooks behind mine and she pushes with her weight.

Only one place to go now.

I topple over as if I have been cut down by a logger, my center of gravity too elevated and now compromised. We clatter onto the ground. Snow unavoidably enters nostrils, jacket sleeves, and pant legs alike, the dog jumps back in pure fear, and my whole body becomes a landing pad. Normally anyone falling on me would be enough to push the wind out of my body but for whatever reason this collapse feels effortless, guided, and uncommonly comfortable. Long brown strands of hair now cover my face and a laughter swells from her belly and into mine. I can't stop laughing.

"It's been too long, dear."

"I know. Only a few days." She says and snorts a little bit in my ear, which would have driven me insane if it was anyone else. Her voice reaches a height where the long consonants still register a heavy tone yet elation flutters her voice high above me, only to dip into the deeper timbres upon each ecstatic inhale. I grab some snow to stuff a handful into her face. She bites it with the crisp regularity of a fresh apple. A joke morphs into a blessing.

So the prank turns on me. She opens her mouth, the final particles melt off her lips and tongue, and trickle onto my face. Credit due when someone turns a prank back on you. If this took place anywhere else with anyone else I would be furious and disgusted. This is far too hilarious for anger, too gross to get mad about. She laughs again in my ear, too loud, but it is OK, I can't fall out of love at that volume.

"Roger promise me one thing..." She whispers barely above audible, her tongue circling the outside of my ear.

"What?" I can barely speak.

"Don't look back."

"OK." She uses my forehead as a push-off point and my ears fill with snow. So lovely. But as she stands up I admire her beauty from a different angle. This only proves beauty to be intrinsic to humanity, an essential function of our species. The sun sneaks through the foggy haze, casting a silhouette, the blinding interaction of limbs, sunlight, and body contours. The sunlight blazes behind her to reveal the delicate form of expression in her fingernails, the divide between her knees and quadriceps a pointed revelation in the romance of the human body with itself. Now I understand when the word "sublime" was first coined. Viewing this.

"Let's go." We have somewhere else to be. And she throws some snow at me, taking advantage of my smitten state.

"We have to be somewhere else?"

"Well, you can just sit here longer if you would like. I won't force you."

"That's one thing I like about you, Adri."

"That I won't force you? I just haven't had the chance to today." She puts her arm out and I grab for it, a light counterweight as I elevate myself. I snow-dust my body to reveal ice chunks all over my hair and down my back.

"You know which path to take, right?" she says. "The right one?"

"Yes, Roger. The right one." A small, wet cloud of snow emerges from her feet as she dashes to the right. "See you where we're supposed to be!" she calls into the wind stream behind her, the thump of feet in snow accelerating as the path tapers downwards.

Where we're supposed to be. Where's that?

I gaze down the path she did not choose. Hazy and darker towards the end, the table and chairs rest far down the foreboding lane. Much further than I remembered from a few minutes or hours ago, however long I've been there. Snow has all but densely enclosed the furniture.

The other trail, far narrower than its counterpart, sits several feet away. The evergreen branches impede easy movement on the trail, elevating Adrianna's run into a far more impressive stratosphere. I don't know why she chose this path but it feels inevitable that I will follow, step by step, the whole journey.

I drop to a knee and put a hand against my leg. The dog sways its tail and mopes her way over to rub her face against my leg. In the next thirty seconds I rub its nose, ears, and pat its back avidly. Dogs have moods as well and this lonely soul pants with renewed invigoration. Maybe I had a helping hand. The wind whips into an enraged severity, and the ground churns under the torrent and lifts pads of snow into the air, dispersing into rival deluges that coagulate to smack me on the back. Now I get why, in myth and story, harsh elements are labeled furies. The dog barks twice and runs down the darker pathway. The weather appears easier down that road, despite what I have experienced.

Yet the way Adrianna took makes the dark path look easier. Her footsteps leave faint outlines in the snow, her speedy gait revealed. But how she followed this path is beyond me. The evergreens smack my face with each step as the trail narrows. Trees have fastened together hundreds of feet above me and the density of the canopy above me darkens the pathway. I let out a little hoot and hear it echo around me. The path must be longer than I thought.

Honestly I cannot tell you how she made it through here. I already lost the original path. Not to the melted ice, wind, or broken branches. Nothing resembles a trail. If someone had laid a trail years before us it is lost to time, long overrun by shrubs and more. Her gait remains expansive, each footstep several feet ahead of the other, as if she skipped or jumped from spot to spot. The consistent snowfall whips up to the pace of a severe storm and I have to pull my jacket tighter, cinch my hood across my face, and keep my head down, focused on the ground, searching for the depressions in the snow that only small human boots can create. At this rate, plowing my legs and arms through the increasing foliage feels more like a swim as I pull myself past brush and fallen tree.

I extend my hands outwards through an exceptionally tight knot of branches and eventually feel nothing. Plopping out on the other side, I see the exterior of a wooden edifice, resembling a front porch. The wood edifice extends high above me until I see an overhang that prevents the snow from engulfing the entrance. From what must be twenty or thirty feet high, the icicles drip onto my head and splatter on the floor. The door appears carved out of the wall itself, nary a wood grain out of place, as if a laser had chosen to cut this rectangle of wood with utmost precision. The metal door handle curves around, an intricate style from hundreds of years ago. I dust the snow off my whole body, turn the handle, and push the door to go inside.

Apparently this place has the works. A fire rages in the far corner deep inside a monolithic fireplace, the andirons larger than the logs themselves The metal grate in front lets the fire tease its way into the large open space, the accompanying ash collecting in a pile below. A regal collection of knits and furs carpet the floor, a meticulously crafted wooden bed is situated to my right, and a coat hanger is right next to me. A long table to my left contains a feast, complete with suckling pig, pots of mashed potatoes and sweet potatoes, and several loaves of bread. I cannot say I'm hungry, but it sure looks good.

Adrianna cannot be found but her outer gear has been flung everywhere. I'm a bit more meticulous. The jacket gets carefully hung on the coat hanger, my boots go outside after I remove them, and my gloves are hung next to the fireplace. I scan the room briefly to find her. I check the bathroom (her favorite hiding spot) then move my way to the table, which remains vacant under the long pews that extend its full length. I check the bed. Nothing. She has a tendency to pull pranks and I have a tendency to remain gullible, no matter who it is, susceptible to the most commonplace trick. Even little girls get the best of me in peekaboo. Older ones?

Are even better.

"Gotcha!" A door I didn't see bursts open behind me. I am tackled and ensnared all at once. I fall for the second time today, this time face first. Thankfully I fall on some plush, ruffled rug that absorbs the pressure on my knees and back. I feel her weight on top of me and I let myself get pinned, both arms extending outwards and fingers stretch into the furthest threads of fabric. She stretches out my hands and holds me to the ground.

"You're getting good at this."

"Thanks, you sweet man. Are you comfortable?"

"Not really, but whatever you have on top of me," and I wiggle my body, lightly shaking her off of my hunched back, "is really really soft. Like too soft. Too comfortable. Too sensualllll."

I feel a pop in my back. Her hands compress on one of my vertebrae and the weight is gone. I spin around to see a fur draped over her shoulders with possibly nothing on underneath. I guess she had two cloaks and now one is mine. How convenient.

"You're wearing too much clothing," she scolds. The pouting begins, a beautiful exaggerated level of frustration

"Probably. It's pretty hot in here, ya know. Compared to out there."

"So do what you have to do." And she taps her wrist and pretends to talk on a cell phone while she waits for me. The shirt and pants come off fast and I stand up, thankfully smart enough not to be a complete idiot and stand up naked, but pulling the fur around me. And to be fair, the soft bear fur retains comfort at a level far superior than the heavy pants and long-sleeved T-shirt. My heart rate skyrockets as I stand, a firm grip on the long sheath of fur, and tiptoe my way to her. She begins to run but I do something she wouldn't dare to do. I toss the bearskin at her, a delicate throw to avoid the fireplace. It misses and lands at her feet. She stops and gazes at me with a sharp smile. She stares at it for a second, smooths out some imperfections, and then sits on the fluffiest part. Her slack-jawed gaze comes from her shock at my willing nudity.

"Nice throw." I nod in reply. I avoid all temptations to be silly and instead take a seat next to her. She puts her hands on the edges of my shoulders and drops her pelt as well. I was right, she chose to wear less than expected. Sweat glistens from armpit to breast to collarbone. Playtime had its effects. Sublime was earlier, but now this? She rests her head on my shoulder and cuddles up next to me in front of the fire. "Roger."

"Yes, Adrianna?"

"I forgot to finish what I said. When you find me, don't look back." She points at herself and mouths "Me." She puts my hand in between her breasts, her skin goosebumping as my two cold fingers touch her sternum. She moves these digits to trace small letters on her body. C O S T....

Everything flashes blue. The lights go off entirely. The darkness hits again and I have lost control of my muscles. Time to wait.

CHAPTER

The bed is still cold, the climate control habitat kept around 68 degrees. I feel invigorated like I always do but this time I know better. I have to keep my reactions no different than before if I really want to pull this off. I look up and the attendant, Jim, sits by my side, a lapdog waiting for his turn for attention.

"Good morning, sir." He extends his hand to help me out of the habitat and tries to hand me the juice. That green juice, again, that is supposed to restore me to after a night of "sleep." A plate of food sits nearby, my favorite egg-white omelette awaiting consumption.

"Good morning, Jim. Nice to see you this Saturday morning."

"Nice to see you too, Mr. Escobar. Just to let you know...."

"Give me a few minutes. I feel a bit woozy." I put up my hand to prevent the glass from being placed in my grasp. I shudder for a second. "Jim, I really need to use the facilities. Could you bring the food into the changing room for me while I take a shower? I'm not feeling too hot and we can talk more after I wash up a little."

"Of course, Mr. Escobar. Just to let you know, it's a simmering 145 degrees in the sun outside today. In the shade it is only 85, and of course, your car has been kept climate-controlled at 75 degrees."

"Thanks, Jim. Give me a minute or two." I try to regain my balance before a sip of the juice. My feet are numb. Some chemical must course through my body since my abstinence from the initial jolt of vitamin C has slowed me down. I cannot handle these steps without help. Jim notices and I have to take his hand.

"You should drink the juice..."

"I will. I am hungry, Jim. But I really need to take a piss. Just help me get there, I feel sore all over."

"Sure thing, sir. But the juice will bring you back faster. Just have at least half. Surely you can wait a few seconds..."

"Fine," I say as I grab the glass with my other hand and drink about half of it. It feels runny and thick, weighed down. I let part of what I brought in my mouth trickle down the inside of the glass, to allow my saliva to mix with the vitamin-and-fruit composition. When the results are taken they should show the reactions of body fluids and juice. I give the glass back to him and he gently guides each of my steps until I reach the locker room.

"Can you just leave the food and drink by my locker? I just want to pee and shower fast before I eat."

"Of course, sir, no problem." He sets the glass on the wooden bench that runs in between the lockers and leaves to get the omelette. I go to the locker and work on the combination quickly... 4 - 8 - 15... and push my pants out of the way to reach the inner sections of my jacket. I touch around the folds and find two syringes. Flattening my hand out, I push from the bottom up and the plastic-tipped needles expose themselves. I gently select one, remove the plastic casing from the tip, and pump air in and out of the chamber. I force the pump handle in to create the vacuum and grab the glass to hold it in my locker. I stick the plunger as far as I can – the needle touches the bottom depth and skitters against the smooth bottom. I pull.

Don't look back.

I drink the rest of the juice in one gulp, put the glass behind me, recap the needle, and force it into my jacket. I untie the strings of the pajamas, which fall off my body. My underwear follows. I spend a minute or two to remove the compresses and bandages around the wound. I grab the bathrobe and toss it over my shoulder as I walk to the shower. The water feels noticeably less refreshing than my last experience. Maybe this is because I didn't finish the juice. Or it's because I haven't eaten. Or because the whole experience was shorter than expected. The shampoo remains wonderful, the soap delightful, yet something is amiss.

While washing myself I examine my leg for the first time in what feels like years, even though only yesterday I had passed Heather's final test. The skin retains a brittle compaction from no water or actual hydration for the past twenty-four hours. But now, under the flow of water, it feels immaculate. That or I still lack the capacity to use my senses to their fullest. I have to say, I think it's the latter.

After the shower I move back to the lockers to find the omelette. I hear frantic footsteps outside – that must be Jim, impatient, deciding on the correct time to tell me I have been suspended for the next few weeks. I know that's coming now. They have coordinated to be ready for my every action and reaction when I'm asleep, so it seems obvious. I reach into my locker and find the second needle. Remove plastic, push the pump, stretch my skin, insert into vein, draw a tiny amount... recap, put back in the jacket. I pinch off a part of the omelette and casually deposit a chunk in the plastic case I concealed in the lower breast pocket.

There. Accomplished.

My black suit sits in the locker covered by a plastic sheath. A uniform ready for the day. That doesn't feel like the right outfit to wear. Unlike most visits, I brought a different change of clothes in a duffel bag. Jeans and a sweatshirt, some comfortable shoes. I don't really have any plans for the day and I never get to wear anything this casual. I stuff my jacket into the duffel bag but leave the suit on the locker rack.

Jim, finally losing patience, comes inside the changing quarters. "Do you need help with anything, sir? You seem a bit slower and still haven't eaten. Those are normally the first two things you do. Is something wrong?"

"I'm not sure, Jim. IS something wrong?" My eyes shoot back a disappointing look. He looks more guilty than me.

"Sir, I hate to say it but you know that this is yet another time that you have broken the rules. Communication during the program – that is not only unnecessary, but pretty foolish as well. We cannot give you any warnings anymore since we have to recalibrate the system for all the damage done. It'll be..." He clicks and touches the screen several times over. "Three weeks until you can return. I hope you are OK with this."

"I'm fine with it. Thanks for the update." I begin to scarf down the omelette, still warm and tasty. Goddamn, I knew I loved this place. The food, the clean clothes... OK. I'm not fine with a ban for three weeks. But I'll try my best to be.

"Can you take the suit to the car for me? I'm just gonna slum it today."

"OK. Just to let you know, last night Michael Murphy left a message."

"He's a friend."

"OK. Well he said to call you when you get out."

"Thanks again, Jim. I'll see you in three weeks."

"Of course, Mr. Escobar. Feel free to drop by at any time."

"I don't think I will, you know, with this suspension."

"Good point. I apologize."

"You did nothing wrong, buddy." I take the duffel and sling it over my shoulder as I walk out to my car. When the attendant slams my door for me, I call Murph. He says he's at the boat. I tell him I'll be there as soon as I can. The office is five minutes from here so I quickly park the car in the loading zone, run upstairs, turn on Dorothy, and tell her to ship the samples off for diagnostics. She seems happy to see me on an off day but I leave as quickly as I arrive. The drive down the freeway goes faster than expected, only ten to fifteen accidents until I reach the marina. When I get there Jane and Murph greet me on the boat with a glass of Champagne. Smiles abound, a toast of thanks for putting them on the list for the Scotch Society. I smile weakly and fall into a chair in the sunlight, the UV rays beating down on me. The nucloud sits on the horizon now – this is the first time I have seen it in a week – and augments the sunset, diffusing gases and heat over the Pacific. The breeze rides in with the waves but reeks of smoke and salt. I can't take it so I ask Jane if I can sit in the main cabin. When I wake up three hours later we are far out at sea, the city no different than the stars far above me, remote and untouchable.

CHAPTER **13**

Today marks day twenty-five of my sobriety. I haven't been able to do much in that time. The first four days were excruciatingly tough. The headaches were awful regardless of my hydration. I paid Heather twice her normal rate to come and stay at the house to make sure I didn't do anything stupid. Well, not stupid. Involuntary.

Let me explain.

When I returned to work the Monday, to no surprise, my test results waited to be opened. They revealed far too much. The drugs that Heather had mentioned were in much larger doses, almost as if they were trying to down a rhinoceros with sedatives and then resuscitate it in under an hour. These drugs, in higher quantities, are available on the streets in most third-world nations. Scopolamine, for instance, remains in use throughout Latin America as a mind-erasing or hypnotic device. The amount I took, in that one visit, would be enough to kill most people. The opiates probably calmed down my reactions and kept my body at a constant heart rate. The amphetamines did what they were supposed to do: keep me alive. Fox methoxy, or 5-methoxy-diisopropyltryptamine, whatever you want to call it, the possible spark for my sexual impulses. They had put together a chemical package that not only worked but had an addictive nature. I wish I could say I enjoyed the addiction. Yet the break from these drugs has been tougher than abstinence from alcohol for any amount of time. Or cigarettes. Or sex.

OK, I'll admit: I have a drink here or there. But we have taken drastic measures for my own safety to ensure I don't escape the condo late at night. I don't know how long I've been locked in this haze. It felt like only twenty visits but now it's forty-six. Those "twenty" visits were over twenty weeks, and by no coincidence at all, those other twenty-six occurred in those same twenty weeks. My body had been inundated with their products. Heather had to be here not just to nurse me back into health, which she did quite well, but also to repress my unconscious desires to go back there, to be animatized back into movement and sent along my way back home after another six- or seven-hour session I can't remember.

Except, now I can. Those sessions just blended into the last. For example, fifteen weeks ago I remember the repetition of "Blue Rondo à la Turk" for what felt like hours before Adrianna's beautiful face hovered over me with a smile that begged me to leave the comfort of my bed. With some help – really, Heather and Dorothy, who we brought back from the office – I've isolated the two instances. I spent seven hours enjoying "Blue Rondo à la Turk" mid-week. And on Friday I heard the end of it, with Adrianna there to start the second sequence. These machinations were put together on me, almost arranged. No different than the lead of a psychologist through therapy. After a circular discussion about yourself for a few sessions, the psychologist will wait to flip your premises on their head. Once he has figured out your justifications and motivations, he removes them. The real work begins.

Yet there weren't just sequences of one dream expanded into two. They have been longer, more devastating. I made Dorothy record and transcribe most of my conversations with Heather. I was too lazy to write it down. The twenty sessions I can remember having with Temporal Dynamic Services "followed" certain patterns. There have been nine major settings used in ten stories. Each have checkpoints and follow an exact narrative structure. It would be far too tedious to list all of them. You would be bored. All are similar, as the company has based them around the initial personality and affections test I took when I first signed up. This means that there were many sequences on the Northern California beaches, several in New Mexico or Mercury, and a few in a cold, icy land that could very well be Minnesota or one of Saturn's moons.

If anything, those were sequences in which I felt most comfortable. I take that back. I haven't been to many of these places. But any truthfully answered questionnaire can reduce a human to mere likes and dislikes. Blue versus red. Hot versus cold. What have you.

But the check marks are there. My behavior has been predicted and watered down to a mere T. This is how they "caught" my attempts to talk to her. When the dosage was lower or as the medication faded away, I would exercise whatever free will I could extend through into my sleep. It wasn't the first time I tried to figure out Adrianna's identity that made them start watching me. Or the second time or the third. They know who she is and maybe I was so far from the truth that it made sense to indulge my fantasy to the fullest. The "Man meets girl, falls in love, lives happily ever after" story, a beautiful script, had a slight impediment. I can never know who she is.

But they underestimated the clever nature of my profession or the training I received. If a lawyer wants to stay in business, they do any and everything for their client. One must know all the possibilities about the situation that the client doesn't know or refuses to know. You have to ask the hard questions. So sometimes the best questions aren't who or what. They are why and where.

Why is a big question, so we focused on the where first. From what little information I got from Adrianna I could extrapolate a narrative. Adrianna is a great name because it translates into nearly every language. Also, I love that name. But her accent, her interactions with me lacked the grace and simplicity of a first-world interaction. She is too elusive, slips in sharper tongues, more sensual and pleasurable than I could have ever expected. I ran my name through various translators to hear how it would sound in almost every Romance language. Then I cross-checked against all dialects, from northern Mexican to Tagalog to Siberian. Her voice – of course, assuming her voice is authentic – appears to contain the tinge of Central American dialects. Her dark skin and raven hair did not exclude her as coming from Europe or the Far East. It's either that or she is Swiss or Welsh, yet her arched eyebrows and distinctly Latin look tell me otherwise.

That doesn't fully answer where. Dorothy is great at that question though. We researched all T.D.S. locations, found every press release, isolated each corporate office, and began to pick apart what made this business tick. Thirty-five locations globally with about fifteen hundred employees. The thirty-five locations are difficult to pin down, but at least eight are in North America, six in Europe, seven between China, Korea, and Japan, and the rest scattered in the major cities in the remaining continents. Maybe six to ten thousand customers, which include men women and children of all varieties of life. A shocking amount of programs exist for the less fortunate to get therapy through the company. These are mostly paid by local governments through mental health subsidies. But anyone could go to T.D.S. provided they met the eligibility requirements. Carpenters. Highway patrolmen. Doctors. Students. Even lawyers. Of which there were barely any. I might be one of ten worldwide.

To some extent, the demographics defied economic lines. The approved customers generally worked as craftsmen and agricultural professionals. The list we made of all the "customers" or "patients" lacked the presence of economic service professionals. You had maybe the occasional regional bank manager from Switzerland, but who is that to anyone, really? I am an anomaly, one of the few legal professionals on the list. I've always felt like an anomaly in life. But I've always felt that whenever I say I'm from this city.

FOREIGN WATERS

Regardless of what draws people to the company, it certainly wasn't THAT expensive. My bills revealed that much. The bill of forty-six visits came out to about a week and a half's salary. Which could be a lot to you, but it really isn't to me anymore. I stopped caring a long time ago. Now T.D.S. have me on the books for so many visits that I can't remember when I've paid them. Maybe the product is different in each country and the Los Angeles location is a high-end version. Mere speculation, I know. But what else could it be?

Back to her though. Each time we tried to communicate in the dream, I only would get a few bits of information. Adrianna only gave me four letters of her last name, C-O-S-T, and three letters of her location, V-E-N. The beginning of the surname is far more open-ended than I would like. The speculation would drive anyone, particularly me, nuts. A multitude of web database searches for all people named "Adrianna COST" under the age of forty-five revealed maybe fifteen thousand different women. One day I decided to click through each and every photo. I prayed for a hopeful stumble upon her instead of blind luck as I sifted through the results. A search engine can only do so much, as they operate on parameters and set designations of words and photos. In this case, we are looking for someone who might be further off the map than I imagined. I believed it would take a human touch to lift her face – the one I see every week – from the bottom of the web's haystack.

It took me five to six hours on the first day to realize I had gone in circles. Or, more accurately, conducted my search the wrong way. Search engines, while great to find products and locations, can only find people who have a presence in the net anyways. And so far she costs me money each day. Her reactions are far more organic, untempered, and without consideration than my trained response of human emotion. Several years ago, when the psychology boards and esteemed collaborators released the paper chronicling fifty-odd years of human interaction with the web, they defined the two crucial characteristics of those who live on the web: a willingness both to be found and to tailor what is found. Her actions lack restraint, a constant unfettered dance with no observers. Except me.

But maybe her actions remain a product of the time we spent together. After all, the entire experience bases itself off a synthetic reality, one imagined, planned, and created to be enjoyed. Her hip twists, hands tugging the tendrils of hair that dangle far below her collarbone – all actions that could exist as a plausible reaction to the unfettered bliss programmed for these, well, almost tangible results. I cannot select, I can only guess.

So a trip across the world makes a lot of sense for this situation. I'll take five, maybe six days off from work. I've already consulted with Dorothy and Heather, who has really grown weary of my presence and "constant whining." They agree that if I have to take a mental health break, at least make a stop near the company's other locations. I wouldn't be the first person to try such a harebrained plan like this on the planet, but I only say that to justify my actions.

FOREIGN WATERS

Maybe there is a better reason why – a determination of self-worth. Most people pursue happiness throughout their entire lives, only to realize that it was all for temporary pleasures. Others pursue money as it bestows them a certain degree of happiness. Beauty grows, then cruelly fades. Sex is cheap and quick satisfaction. The birth of a child justifies any further means to their happiness. Art may be worth everything to you even if it's worth nothing to anyone else. Love conquers all. What have you. All clichés.

Not only can they be right more often than not, but they quantify what we think about humanity in quaint terms. It's easy to believe that it is better to love than be loved – because you can control who or what you loved. It's easy to believe that children justify an existence when you haven't done anything else in your life. It's easier still to validate your life based off a bank account. It's easier still to donate a portion of the paycheck to the charity of your choice, just so your casket has one more person next to it as layer upon layer of earth rests upon your corpse.

I can't put value in any of that anymore. They are unavailable. There must be more to life as so much is unfulfilling. Only now I can accept that I've been lonely for weeks, but truthfully, probably longer. Heather claimed I had the textbook definition of depression, stemming from the loss of a familial unit. So I checked with my friends, the few that remained through the years, and they said I should take a vacation, somewhere, anywhere, that we possibly have friends or people who can show me a great time.

Murph and Jane laughed at the list of places I threw out, as a month ago we had already gone through the list. The T.D.S. location list with V-E-N cities and towns within one hundred miles. Venice, Ventura, Venice Beach, Vienna, Versailles, Vero Beach. Since they both had vacation time from work, they looked at each other and saw opportunity.

"We're coming with you. I know Michael wants a vacation..."

"Badly," he chimed in.

"Well, can we have a good time and not just have you two like making out and me not sitting there saying, 'This sucks, I'm going to the spa.' Only to find you have been there ALL day and now I feel tainted because I just want to relax..."

"Don't worry, dear," cooed Jane as she exhaled some smoke into the camera lens. This was her favorite part about the online chat – hiding behind a cigarette. It was agreed: we would visit Venice, where we would get shitfaced at Harry's Bar more than a few times. I don't care if the Bellinis cost $250 right now, they'd be worth it for the taste and the enjoyment. I really love Venice because some businesses never close there, they just change ownership to make them more profitable with the times. That said, it's still the best Bellini on the planet. From there I could wander the streets and maybe buy art or leer into another bar, maybe smell some cigars, what have you. It would be fun. I would enjoy myself, as would they.

FOREIGN WATERS

The reservations would be easy. Most high-end hotels accommodate the long weekender. My plan was not to pack very much at all. After all, I would rather shop with the money I don't have than save it for an emergency that I hope I won't have. I would take the sturdiest bag I have and fill it with toiletries. Everything else would be bought there. Customs be damned.

So a few days ago I did what I had to do. I dug up the number I had tried to forget throughout my sobriety, yet found it at my fingertips once again. She picked up pretty fast.

"Jules, you have to forgive me. I can't talk to you anymore."

"Why not? What are you doing at the airport?" I guess she figured out I was not at the office. I would hope so. Chatter in multiple languages surrounded me while I tried to make the call go off without a hitch.

"I just can't. Look, I need to make this flight. Maybe we'll talk again, someday. But right now I need to do something else and I need you not calling me. "

"You said we'd never stop talking."

"We both said a lot. And so many things weren't true, or if true then, are not now. I'll fly away, out of sight. Maybe I'll be gone, swept away somewhere else. I don't know why. I'm going to take it as it comes."

"I still want you in my life, Roger."

"I still want **you** in my life, Jules. I always have. But that life was then. That was a different time, a different place. You won't be able to reach me."

"Are you seeing someone else?"

"Not really. Maybe talking."

"You're like every other man at heart, Roger. Can't you stop?"

"Listen. I forgave you months ago. That's why we're talking right now. You already had me, Julia. And I enjoyed every minute of it. We made our nest together, you flew away. I've been stuck living in our memories, in the same condo, in the same job. You left all of that and it was all I had. But now it's not all I have. Now I need my space."

"You can't do that."

"You did it. You've been gone for years. I shouldn't have even called but I felt I should. That's how much I cared – I called my ex-wife to apologize for not talking to her, even after she left me three years ago, without kids, without a home, in a city as cruel as she. But I cared. And now I care about something else."

She said a bunch of words after that and I waited for her to stop the logorrhea before I put down the tablet. I just quietly stared into her eyes. I didn't need to talk to her anymore because we had said enough to each other in our lives already. That subtle realization of aging, that there are so many minutes and hours in the day to talk to someone after you lay eyes on them and smile for the first time. From there, at any time people can choose to end your conversation. And they will. Some conversations die faster than others, others go on for lifetimes. Everyone does it, even me.

So a singular option sat in front me. Keep the dream alive, consider what could have been. Or forget about what it was and think about what life will be. I bought the ticket to Venice before I ever talked to Jane and Murph.

I pressed the top right corner of the tablet screen twice and the device died in my hand. I gently placed it in my duffel bag, put back on my sunglasses, and smoothed out my sweater. Time to get out of here.

Wherever here remains. Don't look back.

CHAPTER **14**

To restart one's life one must begin from the beginning. That means an endless pampering, no different than when one was a newborn baby. Forty-five days off the medications and drugs and I have regained some color in my face, but that wasn't enough to begin a transformation in my soul.

Yes, this was a process of rebirth. To carry empty suitcases into a city of shops and restaurants and spas and tourist traps on bridges, I will let myself succumb to other people's decisions. Yesterday was filled with them.

We arrived in Venice late Thursday night. So Friday we hit the ground running. First up was a proper haircut. I didn't know where to go so I asked the concierge and he pointed me to a little shop down the street. I got a cut and shave, a shot of espresso followed by a glass of wine followed by a glass of water, and then stepped outside. My hair trimmed high up the back of my neck, oiled back and combed with a hard part line. I stepped to my right and got my shoes shined with some dedicated puffs on a *Sigaro Toscano*. I hadn't had these cigars in far too long. Their flavor dry and decisive, typical of a fermented cigar. Of course I can't smoke like I used to but I gave it a try because, well, it's a celebration.

Murph's birthday tonight would be a grand occasion and the three of us took advantage of the whole day to prepare. The flexibility of our lives and friendships let us play a silly game. Instead of purchasing items for ourselves, we bought each other gifts from the markets around the Grand Canal. There was an elaborate process to show off the new apparel and, after a successful strut or two down an imaginary catwalk and a few pouty faces, someone would have to buy it for you. These games only exist because, while Murph came from privilege, Jane did not and spent a good chunk of her life to learn how to convince a man to buy her a gift from the store. So I copied. And Murph eventually caught on. The spending game is fun, especially for those of us who can't afford it.

Item after item purchased, indulgences on vintage gear if it was available. "Better to have the last of something, you know," Jane said with a smirk. I had to agree, that gave more of a reason to take advantage of the game. Buy an object that'll last forever, even if you hardly get to wear it. A fun shirt or hat. I bought her a pair of vintage Pucci glasses. Murph got light blue slacks and light blue shoes to match. He hated the process, pulling on the tight pant legs, a painful moan emanating through the changing room curtain. Jane told him he looked fabulous. I told him he looked "fabulous." The price tag, higher than the sunglasses, was worth the price of embarrassment.

The walk home was brisk but still infernally hot, the famous sun parching the lagoon of St. Mark's Square. Jane found carnival masks for each of us. The delight shimmered off her face when she overpaid for the meager wood carvings. For whatever reason she believed the *baùtta* were the ones to buy. Fun masks, certainly, but lacking the long noses of the famous collector's item. The hotel was a little bit further than the square. The constant creaks, one tiny elevator, and lack of a busy bar could have made this place forgettable. Yet the rooms were immaculate, with pillows and comforters of down, towels of Afghani cotton, and a rare luxury in Venice: silence. The rooftop restaurant couldn't be overlooked as well. A view of the Adriatic, the Lido, and service from the fine ladies and gentlemen of Treviso.

With a quick glance at the time, we realized our reservations were more than a few minutes ago. We retired to our rooms, eager to change into some brand new duds, and had a gondola ready to take us to dinner. An ideal situation, far too much fun for my own good.

We indulged Harry's Bar for about fifteen drinks each. I think you've heard about Harry's. Always a lovely joint. The classic location in Venice hasn't changed much in the past few years. They wanted to throw us out but, somehow, whenever we bought them a drink, they took it. So the party continued. It was fun to rack up a bar tab for several thousand dollars in only a few hours but really, it felt healthy. My friend reminded me that the best peaches are from northern Italy. I reminded him that the best peaches are from Georgia, as are the best cheeks. Everybody seemed to laugh with me and platter after platter came to our table to be consumed in spoonfuls, Bellinis and spoonful of sauces and *grappas* and Bellinis. I could speak Italian pretty well by then. I'd practiced for the past ten hours.

No one wanted to go back home because the night was young. Midnight led to other opportunities. Jane said she had a plan – she wanted to go to this event she heard goes all night in the southern quarter of what is now "new" Venice, built on top of the crumbled edifices that sunk a few years back. Nobody really knew why they sunk, but if you build on top of hundreds-of-years-old waterlogged materials, I believe it could only be inevitable.

Jane asked us to take the intricate *baùtta* masks she bought at the market to the party. Intoxication coupled with disguise – maybe my eyes had blurred from the *grappa*, but everyone looked far different than how I remembered with such a simple mask. It looked far-fetched that we would attend a masquerade, a party she always wanted to throw in their house back in Los Angeles but never did because "Michael here wouldn't want to host a party like that," she said. "You know him Roger, he's a great boy. But he likes to stay straight and narrow far too much."

"I disagree," he burped. "I made Roger some toys for the vacation. Sneaky stuff. For a sneaky guy. How's that for a risk babe."

"Sometimes, Roger, I wish he'd call me a bitch instead," she said in my face, far too loud.

"Whatever, guys. I'm over it. Let's go and see this place. Stop arguing please. Please? Let's have some fun, *buona sera senorita*. Let us enjoy the rest of this night in Venice someway, somehow, and maybe get in some trouble. I need trouble tonight, Jane, so let's make it happen," I said.

She winked. "I gotcha covered, old man. But be ready, you might have to be... daring."

"Whatever you say. Right, Mikey?"

"Buzz off, man, I don't want to leave here any time soon."

"You have to come." She walked over and grabbed him and I reached for the bill and put it on the company card without even a glance. I signed it with a bunch of squiggles that loosely replicated my signature, put my mask on, and began to wander the streets. Murph hadn't lied. He gave me some cards and they were in my pocket. One of them was an identity replicator. This allowed access to locked doors by just pressing a comparable card against the rough side of the replicator. The information transfers and *voilà*! The other was a multi-key generator which basically guesses the 780 million most popular passwords in under three seconds. A nice trick but it can only be used on password-approved entryways, so really, it could be useless. But a useless start is still a start. At least wherever we were going now, it could be useful if I really needed to break in somewhere.

We stopped at a *locanda*, far from the Grand Canal. I guessed this was the newly renovated northern section of the city. My impatience had grown worse because I had not had a drink for fifteen minutes. Mrs. Murphy, dressed in the most stunning combination of black and black and black and more black, walked in unquestioned by the doorman who pointed upstairs. I guess there were more like us.

Up the stairs resided something Michael Murphy never expected.

Jane knocked on the door. Muddled disco music wafted through the door slit. The door swung open after several minutes. We were greeted by a man with a large mustache, aviator glasses, and no shirt. He sized us up and down. I already knew what was up. Murph didn't.

As she slipped through the doorway I followed Jane with all my heart. I put on my blinders and focused on her sloped shoulder, but I could not ignore the rampant sexual prowess that flowed throughout the residence. Groups dominated one another, and, in some cases, were drawn out in all corners of the room. Three or four or five people indulged themselves on any available unused flesh, not everyone masked or clothed or even active in the event. Shrieks of ecstasy and punishment echoed off the walls, sometimes both coupled in the same voice. All forms of sexual persuasions, mostly pain and domination influenced, on display. *Venite se vi piace* etched in wood above the fireplace. Come if you like. Murph entered right behind me and could not believe his own eyes, as revealed by the fire on the far side of the room. Silhouettes shot up and down, scarring my memory as they revealed a depth of repressed perversion. We followed what looked like Jane into the back room where a bar served only red or white wine.

"Red if you're playing for the night." Jane grinned and licked her lips. She looked at us with an expectation of a choice to be made. Murph could hardly believe his eyes. Not that the man was a prude. But he was like his father and I feel confident stating his sex life was as drab as well.

"What if I don't want to play for the night?" I offered.

"Yeah, what if?" asked Murph. His words hung in the air with unnerved dread.

"Is anyone going to choose before me?" She pouted. Jane, in a majestic pose, stunned me with her beauty. The black dress shimmered through the shadows. Then again there is no such thing as too much black. While smashed and beautiful, she looked too pretty to wear so unflattering of a mask. She went to the bartender and pointed to the right. He came back with a glass of red. My jaw dropped.

"Babe, let's leave," Murph said.

"No." She blew him a kiss and winked. "It doesn't mean I want to be with anyone else, babe. It could just mean I want to be with you."

"Or you could be lying."

139

"You think I'd lie?"

"I know you lie."

"Guys, I'd like to get out of here. It might be best if we really leave," I said, in an attempt to diffuse the situation. "I'm a bit of a prude and I need to leave. I can't drink anymore and I feel woozy." Sometimes in life you have to lie.

"Fine," roared Jane and the glass of red wine slammed into table. She knew I tried to cover for him but it didn't matter anymore now. She might be mad at me, him, or herself. I gently placed my glass of white wine next to her and offered her my friendly hand on her arm.

She tore off her mask, threw it into a trash can, and marched off in whatever direction she seemed to fancy best. Michael followed her and I followed Michael. No gondola, no water taxi on the canals around us. Her shoes slung over her shoulders, myself and Murph sweated out alcohol through our fine dinner clothing. After ten minutes she stopped dead in her tracks. The shoes dropped. She held her face with both hands and turned around. Murph walked to her and she asked how to get back to the hotel. He put his arm around her but she shrugged it off. She spit on his shoes.

Exasperated, I pointed to the canal and guessed that if we followed it we would return to the hotel. In under half an hour we had bypassed most of the spots where we shopped earlier in the day.

FOREIGN WATERS

The concierge, both ecstatic and surprised to see us, said I had a message waiting. I told him to hold it for the morning while I escorted the couple back to their bedroom. But I was too late for that. Jane had stomped up the stairs. Murph's shoulders slumped. Their room had a door that opened into mine and I always left mine open because, you know, who knows? It didn't open that night and that was OK. I didn't hear any arguing. Or fighting. Just a cold, cold, cold sob while someone snored blissfully to sleep. I put on the television for a few minutes to phase out the sound. But I passed out face first onto my bed, hoping I told the coffee to arrive at ten instead of nine.

CHAPTER **15**

When I wake up the next morning I have espresso and croissants waiting for me. The true continental breakfast. No noise is heard from the other side of the door. My initial reaction is that they are still asleep, but I know there is no way Murph could sleep silently. I knock on the door and hear nothing.

"Jane? Murph? Anybody?"

All I get is nobody. I guess they got up earlier than me. The copy of USA Today appears swiped from the front of their door. I call the restaurant upstairs and ask them to find the American couple. After a few minutes the waiter returns to say that no American couple had been up there this morning. As confused as I am, that gives me an excuse to make more of this day. Maybe this was the plan all along.

The balmy humidity, a trademark of the Mediterranean climate, feels irrelevant. I have to wear the clothing we bought yesterday. I look like a fool in the same white pants two days in a row but who cares. Thank God I didn't shit myself in the only pants I have. I call the front desk and receive the message. From Dorothy to confirm the location of the T.D.S. service here. It was in the part of "new" Venice I had never visited. Time for exploration.

Really, I have nothing else to do today. With my travel partners nowhere to be found, I have no more excuses.

***

I finally arrive at a gated entryway deep on the other side of a square that boldly displays the logo of T.D.S. The whole thing feels surreal. Behind me sits the entire other half of the city, still held together on its decayed base, and in front of me sits a whole suburb to keep the ruins alive. "New" Venice feels too artificial, out of touch with its parent land. I wait at a cafe on the other side of the plaza and watch as people go in with a keycard no different than the one I used back at home. The guard leans in front of the door and barely checks their badges, if at all. Murph gave me two choices how to handle this situation. I want to try the fun one – a swipe to copy the guard's card and a dash inside. It would take some cunning and some distraction on his part. So I sit and wait and puff another cigar because the focus on breath would make me stronger, more focused, and ready to go. I decide to indulge myself. Two espressos. *Un tartufo*. Chocolate and coffee should never be far from each other.

An hour later he takes a phone call. After a few minutes his face is distorted, an obvious reaction to frustration, and he's gotten agitated. His jacket rests next to the door but he wanders around the corner, obviously to avoid being seen on the street on his company's dime. Even on this new real estate times are tough.

"Going out...," he mumbles in his broken English.

"But I can't stop it, Jenny. You are that American girl, you know?" He stops. Stares at the ground. The conversation changes.

"I'm just, I'm just not innit, at all, people are still there, I envied you, girl. I can't take my eyes off you I can't take my eyes off you I can't take my eyes off you I can't take my eyes off you I can't take my eyes off you I can't take my eyes off you I can't take my eyes off you I envied you girl. I envied you." His voice mere clutter into the cell phone. It seems like whoever is on the other end has the same listening capacity as he. Basically, none at all. He paces back and forth, the concern dripping off his face from the events of this conversation. Finally, a rental cop doing his job properly: doing nothing at all.

I take this as an opportunity to swipe my card twice on his, a double touch to secure the code. I have about fifteen seconds by the time I say this, now ten.

I still can't dash fast but it's just enough and I make it to the guardhouse keycard in time. A quick slap of the card drops me into the center hallway. Male and female locker rooms are only a few feet away. I dip into the male room, the bathrooms doors ajar. The urinals are caked and decrepit. I rummage the place to find any pants and shirt that aren't white and remotely look like they can fit me. Wait a minute. This is easy. Thank God this is Italy. Every suit fits me here, guard or business.

The quick change makes this far more comfortable of an affair. Murph and Jane had tortured me aesthetically last night. A button-down shirt with red cuffs on a lemon print, white pants. Far too obvious. But now I can get to the habitat chambers easily if the layout is as simple as the one back home. It seems like it is. The guards may not know me and I don't really know Italian, but I could say that they placed me here and now I have to look after some patient and BS the whole thing... It's worth a shot. Worst they can do is take me to their leader who probably speaks English anyways to solve everything. Well, screw it, I'll speak Italian if I have to.

"*Buona sera*," I say with a casual wave. I proudly display my new badge to them, all smug and satisfied as a king on a golden pile. They're not agitated by my presence. They just stop me, light a smokeless hash cigarette, and size me up.

"*Qual è il tuo compagno nome? Sei qui per prelevare una persona, o, anche, prendere un po 'di uno?*"

"Buenas tardes. Uno poco espanol por favor." Speaking Italian... farrrrrrrrrr too much for me to handle right now. Time to go to a backup plan. I couldn't understand a word they said. They nod and point to the floor, a nice gesture. "Ahora necesito una mujer para las oficinas de Los Angeles. Una muy fresa y perfecta, ya?" My hands animate the situation as I use whatever broken Spanish I have left to make them get an idea I need to see some of the people.

"*Qualunque cosa, stiamo solo andando a roba che su come l'ultima.*"

"La ultima?" That's the only word I got out of that one. Must be the final one.

"Si, hermano." He winks at me and points down the hall, to the corridor behind the habitats. At the very end there is an open door that has a larger hallway. Jackpot.

"*Bueno.* Gracias... no... *prego!*" And I bow and walk and they wave and laugh and I continue on my way. My feet shuffle down the hallway and I look at the large bays of dormant inhabitants and unused pods ready for the next customer, not much different than the facilities at home. I will say the facilities at home are vastly more refined. The technology seems more versatile and built to last in Los Angeles. But here it feels as if it is built to handle multiple customers around a central staircase. As I walk past the staircase I peek down the central corridor to count the amount of handrails I see on one side. This place must be ten floors deeper than the location back home. What a marvel.

But to build this here, half underwater? That must have been done with some extreme foresight and an impressive ability to bribe local officials. I begin to imagine whole parts of the "present" city, the elevated rooftop construction of New Venice, use part of this structure as a cornerstone. If I had to guess, the whole thing must be two or three football fields long. This floor is at least. Width... much more narrow, like a three-to-one ratio, so let's say about a football-field wide. A clandestine project of this magnitude would take more than a few years to build. To the common man that walks these streets, knowing that this entire operation exists underneath the city would be about as plausible as...

This chamber not existing. As I step into the open doorway and into this thin hallway, the closest chamber kidnaps my eye and then my body and possibly my soul. I don't know why this chamber exists or why it is filled with a wide range of humanity.

Truly a wider range than I ever thought. The first person is the largest of the group of three. He is suspended in the air by a yellow gel that seems to keep the whole body in a comfortable, non-encumbered state. Surprisingly lean, the man has a large clear tube that enters his inner thigh, a liquid pipelined straight into the artery. Several more attach to an arm that twitches incessantly in the goop. The yellow gelatinous mass vibrates on a near-constant basis. It spills over the top of the chamber as the glass constantly rattles. The rest of the body couldn't move if it tried. The headset that every customer wears each night is twice the size and covers the eyes, with two little nostril plugs either to prevent leakage or prevent intake. A nasty scene but graciously lacking a face.

FOREIGN WATERS

The second is a child, which was strange as I have never seen a child in the location back home. The girl, about seven years old, is suspended in a light pink liquid. The top of the container appears to be Tupperware-sealed, yet the glass lightly vibrates as the fluid gently swooshes back and forth. She seems to just follow the current and rotation of the tide. It could be a beautiful scene if it was on a beach off the Lido, ten miles away, but we're here. She isn't wearing what girls her age are supposed to wear, especially with catheters and so forth attached where clothing should be.

I really want to like the third but he is far beyond atrophied, a poor soul with Lou Gehrig's disease that has aged his body without mercy. It would be graceful if it wasn't as if a child's skin had been stretched on an adult skeleton, but it is what it is. Grotesque twitches of the left hand and left are both unnatural to human movement and unbearable simply to watch. About twenty tubes rig themselves to the body, mostly at arterial locations. A metal bar sits below the buttocks to keep the body upright. The pale skin is held in a firmer solution, possibly to prevent the gentle sloughing away into the very fluid that sustains his body position.

And row of three after row of three, a total of ten rows, thirty inhabitants of this chamber. I turn around to exit and dry heave into my mouth. Up and down the hall sit similar doors that probably have identical chambers. Maybe ten of them. I beeline to whichever end is further and march till I reach the wall. Above that chamber door, several geometric designs are stenciled to the door frame alongside an imprint of the whole Asian continent. The door next to this one has several geometric designs as well, far different from the first door, and an imprint of North America. Diversity of assets, a sort of exclusionism... I don't understand the segregation. By the end of the count there are three doors for North America, one for South America, three for Europe, one for Africa, and two for Asia.

I really don't want to walk down each aisle of each one and look because this is probably not where she rests. Who you are in real life can be and generally is always replicated to exact specs in the program. Yet I doubt that the program always works that way. I mean, everything can get altered in any program at any time. I'm sure it can be manipulated to change appearances for certain situations, right?

If I want to keep down the three Nutella croissants and two espressos I had this morning I have to get out of here. This whole hallway contains a vile noxious smell of liquid silica. So I make my way back to the main hall and skim my feet down the length of the central passage. Two doors appear on my right side near the staircase and the guards walk to me, having just rounded the staircase almost as if they want to approach me from the widest possible angle. Their smiles beam a medicated radiance. They're calm yet at the same time cracking jokes to each other. The uniformed gentlemen can't hide that they were laughing at me.

FOREIGN WATERS

"Amigo, amigo, amigo!" one says, greeting me with open arms, jokingly leaning from side to side.

Nothing can remotely prepare for the swift kick to my bad leg that knocks me to my knees. They grab both of my arms and lift me into the air. Instead of an arrest or a pummeling of fists, they would rather paralyze me with machismo. I guess the jig is up. They raise my body high in the air, each shoulder falling into place, my arms pushed at obnoxious angles that would make any movement painful. I try to hit one of them in the head yet I can't rotate my arm at my elbow. All the actions are for naught and at this rate I am better off as a prisoner than the outraged free man. I am a paying customer in this establishment, but any communication would be poor at best.

My decision making is in their hands. I had initially wanted to open the door to the left of the stairs. Instead they take me one floor down, each successive step on the staircase more painful than the next. Each step is untimed between the two men, my joints the only thing keeping my shoulders attached to my arms. They rock in sharp pain as the bones release themselves briefly from the socket, jarred out and into place over and over again. Each step on the staircase looks about two feet long, requiring an elongated gait to make sure it takes one step per stair. Or, really, the equivalent taunt stretch of my shoulders on the rack and slow application of pressure until the bone pops out of its socket, then sliding it back into place, only to repeat it again and again and again.

They open a door and lower me just enough to enter the next doorway. It reeks of cigar smoke, probably due to the poor ventilation in a central room inside such a large edifice. Roaring Twenties jazz creeps out the door. A portly gentleman in a well-cut business suit stares at three large screens –one simply crunching numbers and data, the middle one for word processing, and the final one appearing to contain medical reports. When he hears my body fall to the floor he spins around in his chair, looks down at me, and smiles. He wears brown shoes with a blue suit. I guess this really is Italy. So fashion forward. I stand up fast and dust off the uniform.

"Did you need someone to speak English with, Mr. Escobar?"

"I guess."

"Well, congratulations, you found the one person in the office who can speak to you. Please take a seat." He points to a chair in the corner. An elegant antique reclining tool with a large curved back that extends far above one's head and an intricate patterned cloth on both arm rests. I collect myself so I can gaze across the room while I sit. With some shock I see a box in the corner that has a logo far too familiar to me: Callatero LLC's stamp. Postage from Veracruz, Mexico. I can't make out anything else... but I can't imagine Romero or his family have anything to do with this. He's in Peoria. But his family is there... too? I can't remember.

"Great to hear. So I guess these two guys have to stay in the room?"

"Like those before you, Mr. Escobar, yes, they will stay in the room to provide protection as we have this conversation."

"Those before me?"

"There are many like you here and all across the world."

"Like me?"

"Like you. And like her, Adrianna Costa." The man smiles with prescience. Her last name is Costa.

"Yeah... How did you know?"

"Mr. Escobar, have some faith. You educated, inquisitive man. After setting up every experience between you and her, don't you think we'd see you coming? I cannot believe you tried that ridiculous costume, anyways. You could never pass for a guard." He snorts when he chuckles. He reaches over to his panel and presses a button behind the monitor twice. My chair vibrates and, in mere seconds, the back panel extends out on either side. The two sections curve inwards, over me, meeting each other in the empty space between armrests. I can't get out if I try.

My plan to rescue her has come undone. Now I need a new plan.

One to rescue myself.

CHAPTER **16**

I t doesn't take much time when you're in an unfamiliar place, already injured from a month ago, then injured again a few minutes ago, to notice each heartbeat of adrenaline. I cannot move in this present state but, so restrained, my senses evolve a hyper-awareness of the layout of the room. The air vent rests in a little grate at the top of the ceiling, hence the poor ventilation. A desk deep with multiple screens rests behind it. Most of the screens display vital statistics of various, what I assume to be, deeply catatonic customers. Yet some of the tablets show activity as experienced in the first person. In one a man sits in front of a girl dressed in the barest of lingerie, teasing him. In another a man hacks at a tree with his axe, each swing on the same spot again and again. And another dives casually into a wave break, suspended in the water until he chooses to float on his back to stare at the sky. I finally rest my eyes on the man as he casually cleans his glasses, then the tablets in front of him. He stretches while he stands up, arms and fingers extended outwards.

"OK, but can you at least show her to me?"

"Who?" he asks.

"Adrianna Costa?" I plead.

"Before or after we have a discussion."

155

"Before, please. I need to make sure my eyes haven't deceived me."

"Very well. She is very popular here you know. Your senses... deceive you? Mr. Escobar, don't you know you cannot trust them?" He points at the two men who grabbed my arms. The portly gentleman presses a button and bends over to lace up his shoes. The clamps release my arms and chest and the two guards lift me up again. The door opens and I, with plenty of force, receive a masterful escort down the hall. At about thirty steps we make a left, then a quick right, then another left. The pods to my right and left contain not just one beautiful woman, but one after the next, all engaged in a deep slumber no different than the one I have experienced so many times before. Their bodies twitch and moan, their minds active their body so their fingers crawl their thighs and sides. Back and toes arch and point. We stop and he swipes his card in front of a slightly larger habitat, one larger than the one at home, to key in a password. I can't see the password. The glass top extends outwards and reveals a slender face, black hair, and turned nose. She shifts in her sleep, calm, content, collected.

Adrianna. Real Adrianna.

"Would you like to talk to her?"

"I don't know, can I?"

"If she feels like talking. I wouldn't wake her now though. Maybe later. Interrupting someone during activity could have negative effects on their ability to sleep in the future." He smirks.

"How did she get here?"

"That is a long story. Adrianna... She is something special here in the office. Like I said." He walks around the elevated habitat, the metallic shine and glass resonating off his face. He casually examines her nails and hair. "She isn't from here. She was a part of the exchange many years ago. When her parents gave her to us, she had been addicted to most of the narcotics common to her land. Her parents owned the land swallowed up by a land grab not far from you. Very wealthy bunch, especially after they decided to negotiate and not deal with the gangsters or cartels. That area. Such a prime spot to harvest the materials that engulf so many addicts such as herself."

"What was she addicted to?" I ask.

"A drug cocktail not too different than the one we give you each evening. That part of the world... There are too many addicts. The problem with the mixture, of course, is its irreversible nature. Not unlike the 2-CE or MDA products out there, HPPD follows continuous usage."

"HPPD?"

"Hallucinogen persisting perception disorder."

"Wait a minute. Drug cocktail?" I remember the box in the office. Callatero LLC... Romero's shell company delivered it. I thought the shell company was only there for charity. "Land grab" is a nice way of putting the creation of the fifty-second state, especially all the violence that surrounded it. I never really followed up much further since I set up the charity. It was for supposed to be for charity, but it was a joke from the start. What did his family members do?

I made a mistake. I didn't do my research. Shit. If I had to guess, Romero's family didn't just shut down the business. His personal accounts must not have been simply for his own use. The charity idea I had was a great front for his whole family. Business must be booming with a client like this one. And when I went to San Diego... I must have helped him get free of any suspicion by the police. Some luck. That wasn't interest falling into his pocket. That was income. His family helped supply these drugs to the only legal buyer: a company supported by two governments to brainwash and drug innocent people. I had been played for a fool.

That's why the box is here. That's why she is here. And, now, that's why I am here.

I am a fool.

"I'm sure you understand now that you aren't exactly sleeping when you use the services of the Los Angeles facility, correct?"

"Correct," I lie. He gestures to the two guards and they grab my arms again. This action immobilizes me in the air. They lift me high. He types in the password, swipes his card, and closes the chamber. He puts his hands on top of the habitat and looks at me.

"Each night you are pumped full of enough medication to keep you in a state of lucid dreaming. Obviously we need a large supply of the materials to operate this business. Thankfully your government and other governments contribute to the advancing costs of research and unplanned expenses." A few flicks of his hand towards the guard and the portly gentleman shuffles his feet back around me to lead us in the direction of the room. We follow, thankfully with less pain than before. My joints must have opened up from the previous expedition.

"What is your business, then? I just thought I was getting a date," I say, squeezing the words out of my lungs.

"Do you really want this?" he says, puffs of smoke emanate from the cigar, unfairly subjecting all of us to an activity that would be illegal in my home county, state, and country. "In the long run it won't matter. You know, whatever I tell you doesn't matter."

"Well, I could sit here and ask a bunch of unrelated questions. Like what's your favorite meal? But I'd rather talk about something important," I say. The cigar fumes into my nose. The men deposit me back in the chair. They hold me in place until he presses the button again. The clamps come on, and thankfully, since I had lost some weight from not drinking so much, I sink a bit further in the chair I expect.

"Hah. Important. You think you know what is important. Something to smoke?" He points at the box of cigars. I shake my head no. He makes himself comfortable, shoving his chair into the table. As it bounces back with a spin, he grabs it and hoists his body into the padded curved seat. "Nobody needs anything other than food and water and a place to shit," he continues. "What makes you any different?"

"What makes me the same?"

"Everyone's the same. That's the point. You, me, not that much apart. But in a place like this? We are exactly the same! Flesh and bone. Water-filled beasts focused on breathing. Temporal Dynamic Services is a business, yes, but not just any business. We picked locations based off of provincial strengths, enticed people based off their temperament and desires, and thought constantly about what might remain when the next ten years pass. And what is necessary after that." His gaunt face lacks expression, compounding my confusion. He presses the button to open the door and the guards slink away behind me.

"Ten years?"

"Look." He pulls out a small box and it projects onto the wall a small map of my hometown. "Do you know how many people died in Los Angeles as the nucloud passed over you?" He presses a button and the nucloud appears from the northeast, a slow crawl from that valley side of the projection to the western coastline.

"No."

"Fifty-five thousand and a handful, Mr. Escobar. But you were fine. You didn't even know it happened other than when you saw it yourself. And that's just the first few years of its existence on this planet. When L.A. has been hit four times, what happens with your kids?" With a cool exhale he shakes his head. "What then? We live in an already frightened world, contaminated by epidemics and now possibly unsolvable ecological difficulties. More is coming. A lot is at stake."

"To our frightened world."

"Yes." He nods. "You are here... Well let me be accurate, you and those before you are here to make sure that when that happens there are people like you present. There will be blood for many years, not just man killing man. A sky rebelling against us, the water losing drinkability. Some people will live through the bloodshed..."

"But most won't."

"And some will be here, locked away, until that time passes."

My eyes stroll back and forth, checking the dials and the switches and the tablets as they blink at me. A far-too-real scenario for comprehension, too exact. This T.D.S. center, so massive and hidden from society, contains a whole society within it. Almost three dozen of these strewn across the globe, all strategically placed. So many lives of so many people. Too many outside who will die.

"What's with the people who are in captivity?"

"You mean the big cases?"

"Yeah. In that other room those assholes let me walk into."

He laughs. "Oh, Mr. Escobar. To be fair, they need something to laugh about. They are the backup generators behind your grand evenings, my friend. We have to swap people in and out sometimes, you know."

"So sometimes I'm not dreaming with Adrianna?"

"In your case, it is her. It has to be. She is not as enfeebled as those you saw before the guards brought you to me. And to be fair," he smiles, "you're far more suspicious than our normal customer."

"There's only ten lawyers. I checked."

"You did your homework well. I shouldn't have been surprised. But yes, you are right. As we say where I am from, *La répétition est la mère de la mémoire.*"

"Huh?"

"I thought you had studied French in the past? It means, repetition is the mother of memory."

"So once you drill it into my head enough, I have to believe. I guess I question too much for my own good and make your job much harder. Where are you from anyways, France?"

"No, Mr. Escobar. Switzerland. And you don't question too much. You make my job exist. That's why the product is based upon choices. So when you do have to take a long sleep, the program already will be adapted to keep you in the mode that you enjoy, making the decisions you like, with the interactions you appreciate. You are a special case, a restless sleeper who questions. My job is to make an environment people like you will enjoy without questioning it."

"Without questioning it? I didn't know I was questioning anything."

"Yes. You may not realize it, Mr. Escobar. Very few can perceive the flaws in the system, even less can exploit it. You exploited your disbelief to find out more of Adrianna. So our circumstance changes. We have to control your questioning. A constant challenge, of course. But progress ensures the safety of the program. Not different than what we have to do today."

"Which is?"

"Well, you found the other half of your match in our system. You can't take her from here and be useful to us at the same time. Other people have tried in the past and some have been reacclimated to society, but others have lost more than their sanity. We knew you would come here eventually, or at least to one of the locations. But your first guess was very good, sir. You hit the nail on the head."

"So why am I here?"

"We're getting you **ready**."

An answer that really couldn't be a lie. "So... I guess I'll play along." I don't have a choice.

"A good answer. Much easier for all of us than the alternatives." The clamps come down harder than before and I feel the entire chair rumble. "I have to tell you... Well, if we talk again, that will be unfortunate. But after this, go find your friends. OK?"

"Sure. Whatever."

He smiles, stands up, leaves the room. The chest piece feels like a harness as I try to break free. I feel for my pockets but my hands cannot reach my legs or the key card Murph gave me. The metal too solid to hammer out any differences and I slam my arms hard up and down to try and burst the whole chair off of me.

I am not that strong.

FOREIGN WATERS

Two guards come in and apply a thick smudge of brown paste underneath my nose. It hits instantly, a noxious intoxication that feels far too familiar. They place their hands under my shoulders. One presses a button and all the clamps release their grips. The men don't. I try to raise my hands but the air, the currents in the air are too strong and my hands flop back down. I get dragged slowly out of the chair with extra care given to my head. The men hold me at a comfortable angle. I know where I am going to go. I only have a few seconds to see that I am placed in a habitat, not far from her, and I might have to navigate through some uncharted waters, maybe a different setting than the times before. As I see her in the habitat, four aisles away, all I can think is that she's already somewhere else and I am about to dream in a new place without her. And the headset, a larger headset, slowly glides over my head. I look down at my hand. My eyes close but I still try to see, an attempt to cling to all fragments of the awakened state. I begin to stare at a star through the clouds, or pieces of my veins through my eyelids, and pick apart the patterns. So many stars. I begin to count them. Over and over again.

To be continued.

Acknowledgments

Special thanks to the beta readers. You know who you are. To the following people who helped me overtly or without ever knowing - J.G. A.V. A.L. S.E. S.D. M.S. P.S.C. J.A. A.C. O.G. R.J. H.H. T.V.N.G. Y.M S.W. B.S. K.F. H.R. A.R. K.K. B.R. W.O. S.A. Y.N.W.A.

FOREIGN WATERS PART 2 – 2014

-

STAY INFORMED

-

VISIT

ALECROJAS.COM

FOR UPDATES

www.ingramcontent.com/pod-product-compliance
Lightning Source LLC
Chambersburg PA
CBHW070327130626
46556CB00007B/2755